I0664883

You Are My Lady

DreamfieldsGrandNanny,*Inc.*

Published by: DreamfieldsGrandNanny, Inc.
8101 Sunrise Lakes Dr. N, #302Sunrise, Fl. 33322
954-695-8042
E-mail::imogenef@aol .com

ISBN#09749959-4-0-

By
Jean Ferguson

About the Author

Imogene (Jean) Ferguson is a native South Carolinian transplanted to Brooklyn, New York in her teens. She educated herself and five children there and until her retirement to Ft. Lauderdale, Florida, was convinced that New York City was the most interesting and exciting place to live and work.

She has held a variety of jobs; sleep-in girl, domestic, survey interviewer, postal clerk, gypsy cab driver/owner, youth coordinator, poll inspector/coordinator, and radio talk show host. She retired from the city of New York as a caseworker and has reinvented herself as a realtor, voter service technician, author and small business owner.

Jean is a community activist and a strong advocate for youth. She is a Christian and believes that God brought her husband (Eric) into her life at a critical time of development and change for her family. He is one of the models for Jason, one of her leading characters. She leads a life filled with family, friends and strangers in need.

JAYNE is her first novel and her fictional autobiography. It is the story of a woman who overcame great odds to successfully educate herself and raise her children. She also wrote and published the autobiography of her extraordinary friend, Mary Glover Pinkett, the first black woman elected to the NYC Council. Her next book; Pure Imogene Perspectives and Pearls is her unabridged autobiography and will be will be available in the winter of 2011.

Thank You

The following people are as much a part of my writing as the paper and ink. I cannot tell you often enough how important your enthusiasm, editing, technical assistance, faith, e -mails, words of encouragement and love means to me.

I need all of the above, (among many more) to keep me writing and on track.

Charlotte Brock-Aguilar, Floyd and Rosie Antonio, Christina Baldwin-El†, Jon .Baldwin, Sr., Karen Black-Barron, Mary Leach-Brown, Robert and Helen Carter, Kerns Conzi, Sharon Crum, Hazel Embden, Eric Hugh Ferguson, Justin D. Fleming, Lucille Gambrell, Dora Garibaldi, Otis B. Gowens, M. Dwayne Herron, Grace M. Herron, Rev. Dr. Melville B. Herron, Gilbert James, Gwen Johnson, Ruby Johnson†, Sor. Corine King, Pauline LaPlante, Cary Lewis, Phoebe J. MacLaughlin, Mama Margot Major, Deborah Stewart, William and Marilyn Lewis, Mama Willia Mae Robinson -Lewis, Robert McCalla, Lillian Pelham, Dennis Quallo, Leslie Rhoden, Betty Robinson, Marilyn Sockwell, Jessie Stringfield, and Celia 'Afia" Wickham.

You Are My Lady

Table of Contents

Bonus Bits and Pieces

You Are My Lady!

Chapter 1

I've always wondered about some of my friends and tried to analyze their relationships with their significant others. I don't mean my married friends, because I long ago decided that what you saw with most married couples, was not what really was and unless I was planning to go into counseling, those relationships were not to be even though on.

The other tag I was curious about often belonged to "the other woman." In my innocence and naïveté, I wondered how could it be possible for a happily married man to fall in love with another woman? Why would a man with a perfectly lovely wife at home even notice another woman? What kind of man can love two women at the same time and sustain a satisfying relationship with both? After all we were no longer living in medieval times.

Women and men are made differently and even though a woman can often fake passion and get away with it, a man could not always fake it (if you know what I mean). And, I told myself; he couldn't really love her (the other woman). He could only be using girlfriend, only setting her up for a serious fall. After all, few men left their wives for their girlfriends, no matter what they told these poor women. After all wives did not pop off conveniently for the lover's convenience.

I tried to get up on a moral high horse and wonder about the woman.

What could she be thinking of to disrespect another sister like that? Didn't girlfriend have any respect for herself? She obviously had major problems with self-esteem, or she just couldn't get a man of her own. I used to get off on those pitiful, needy, lonely, frustrated and often, gorgeous creatures. She might look all right, but surely girlfriend must not know it if she needed someone else's husband to boost her self-esteem.

If she were all that confident, she'd do better than some old married man. I felt so superior to them (my hapless friends) after all I was married, had a good job and had proven my womanhood by having a couple of beautiful, intelligent children. I know I still looked good (at least fifteen years younger than my age) and the body was still firm, a size eighteen, but seriously firm. After twenty years of the same job, the same gym and the same man, I was feeling pretty doggoned smug and more than a little sanctimonious. That is until Gus exploded into my life and my libido.

One minute I was taking care of my house, putting up with my husband and letting my daughters drive me mad. My car was even running all right for a change. I was in the midst of a business conference that I had worked my heart out and butt on, and one that would ensure my professional security.

The next moment my whole world had come to an abrupt halt. I was in the grip of feelings I could have sworn were dead and buried. I felt like a well-dressed Mack truck had rolled right over me. My chest hurt and I could literally feel a curious but delicious pang centered somewhere below my waist. I want to tell you that I was rocked emotionally and physically and at a loss to do anything about it.

As I said, I was in the midst of a three- day business conference held at the Crowne Plaza Hotel near LaGuardia Airport. This girl was booked into the Governor Suite at my company's expense, because as vice president of marketing, the conference was my baby. I had fifty of the computer field's brightest and best, listening to me project our five - year plan for expansion and holding our share of the computer market.

I had worked around-the-clock, seven days a week for the past two months to prepare my staff and myself for this conference. I knew the effort was paying off. I had their attention and my boss (Jake Ames) was preening like he had something to do with it. There wouldn't be a promotion out of this, but maybe I could work a cash bonus large enough for a two-week vacation at the Jamaica Grande in Ocho Rios for Hugh and myself. We both loved Jamaica and this could buy us a few days in Paradise.

On Saturday evening, the company threw a cocktail party in my suite, complete with music and a loaded bar. I was so tired I got my Pina Colada and stepped out onto the terrace, where I leaned up against the rail and closed my eyes. There was a fuel-tinted breeze blowing from the direction of the airport and a jet took off, leaving me wondering idly where it was headed. I was tired but exhilarated and I must admit to feeling a little smug. I had pulled this thing off; with my know how, backed up by sheer guts and attention to every, single tiny detail. I, Carmen had made this weekend a success.

As I opened my eyes I felt someone watching me from the doorway. As I turned, my own eyes connected with a pair of warm, velvety brown ones, shaded by the most gorgeous lashes I'd ever seen on a man. A long, masculine nose saved his face from being too pretty and he had the kind of compact build and neat behind that I've always loved on a man.

He was standing there in the doorway staring at me as if he'd seen his Mama, knowing she had been dead for many years. My heart dipped into the lower regions of my belly and I knew my face was suffused with her. He blinked as if to clear his vision and I mentally stumbled; I unconsciously reached for my balance.

As he turned back into the room, I felt as though I'd lost my best friend. I almost reached out my hand to him in entreaty but instead shook myself mentally and took a long sip of my drink. The evening had suddenly turned just as flat. It was as if all the color had drained out of the sunset and my life and left it gray.

I pasted on my brightest smile and went back inside to play hostess. As I chatted with my guests, I scanned the room out of the corner of my eye. There was not another pair of dark velvety, heart-stopping eyes to be found in that room. I joined a group of colleagues in the sitting area and talked shop for a while and found that I could not settle down. After awhile I finally gave it up and headed for the terrace, where I could be alone with my unsettling thoughts and maybe relive that dream painted into my consciousness.

As I stood by the rail and watched a jet take off, I had an inexplicable feeling that a part of me had taken off too, a part that I would not get back. Something momentous had happened in those few seconds. I quietly waited for the air to settle around me. When I felt that I could move again I stepped back into the room and continued my hostess duties.

I knew that the conference was a success. I also knew that something had happened that was way beyond my control and I liked to be in control. Not just personally, but in every aspect of my life. On a personal level there was Hugh and the girls to be dealt with. On a business level, I was at the top of my game. I knew just how hard I would have to work to stay there. My boss, Jake Ames had placed his confidence in me. I was pretty sure that he would be proud of the work I had done this weekend.

Meanwhile I needed to get back to my guests, and pack up my materials and equipment. I wanted to get home as soon as possible to check on Shawn. I knew I had to take that situation I hand too. I might as well get started straightening those young folk out.

Gus let himself into the back door of the house. He felt his way by instinct to the kitchen where a small light glowed over the sink. The sink was placed under a wide window nearly covered with hanging plants and overlooked the backyard and garden. He always stopped there on his way into the house. Gus loved his lawn and garden and spent many satisfying hours mowing his lawn and working in his garden. His Jamaican roots lay in his hands, and working in the earth gave him a great deal of satisfaction.

The view through the window should have calmed him and restored his equilibrium. Tonight the moonlight softly shining on the shrubs and lawn only served to highlight his inner turbulence. "What in the hell just happened out there," he asked himself? "I have not felt like this about any women since I met Candace."

" Come on man, be honest with yourself," he argued inwardly. "All right, I have never felt like that before, period. Why do I have the feeling that I have just escaped from something inevitable? I know one thing, I got out of there just in time. Maybe a brandy will help calm me down," he thought. "Something had better before I go upstairs to my wife."

He walked over to the bar built into the corner of the living room and without a thought of warning the balloon, poured a hefty slug of Napoleon brandy into the glass. The brandy burned its way down his throat into his chest, leaving a trail of fire in its wake. That fire matched the one that had started in his gut at the sight of that sexy, earthy dream woman in the electric blue suit. The view of her standing at the rail of the terrace, backlit by the setting sun over Manhattan, burned itself in his brain. It also burned itself in another part of his anatomy. That place, he would rather not think about. Her shimmering image blazed across his mind in much the same way as the brandy blazed a path through his chest. He shook his head to clear his vision, but she was still there, so he took another swallow of his drink.

The fire didn't blaze as brightly this time and the image blurred just a little. After the third, slower sip of his drink he felt calm enough to go upstairs. He rinsed his glass, put out the lights and slowly headed for the stairs. "Gus, where were you? Since you didn't call I waited supper. What happened, did you get held up at the office?" Candace sat up in bed as she spoke to her husband.

"I stopped in at the cocktail party given by one of my customers. I thought I had told you earlier in the week that I would be late tonight." Gus said to his childhood sweetheart and wife of thirty years. She looked like a teenager with her hair falling around her shoulders and her flannel nightgown buttoned up to her neck. "Maybe you did, but I forgot. Did you enjoy yourself?"

"Not really, but I showed my face and actually made some contacts. I don't really like these things, even though they're good for business. I'd much rather go out with people I know."

"You mean with your Lodge brothers, don't you?" Candace couldn't help but get that one in. she was more than a little weary of Gus and his brothers'. He had been a Mason when they got married. At first it was fun getting all dressed up and attending the various social functions together. They got many compliments: especially as they danced together. At first she had enjoyed the attention. After the children were born, it was a hassle getting dressed up and finding a babysitter every weekend. After a while Gus had started going alone. Some of the older women had advised her to find a way to go with him, as some other woman would snap him up once they realized he was virtually single.

She ignored them because she knew that Gus loved her and that he was a man of honor. He would never do anything to jeopardize their marriage or betray their vows. Her husband happened to be one of the few honorable men she knew. It was an open secret that several of the men in their social set had mistresses, or long standing girlfriends. Their wives knew about the women but chose to ignore the liaisons. Some of her women friends even had lovers, but her Gus had never so much as looked at another woman. Sometimes she wished he were not so honorable, it made her secret so much more difficult to bear.

Even though she was no longer really interested, they still had a sex life. It was based mainly on when she felt like it. It had been awhile since they'd had sex. Maybe I'd better make an effort tonight," she thought. "Gus honey, why don't you come to bed? I've been waiting up for you."

"I'll be right there baby," he called from the shower. "I'm not up to this tonight," he thought to himself as an image of Carmen flashed through his head. He came out of the bathroom toweling his chest dry. "Come here Honey and let me do that," Candace called to him from the bed. "I haven't dried you off in a long time."

This was truly one of the things she did not mind doing still. Candace had always loved rubbing her face cat-like against his furry chest and listening to his strong heartbeat. There was something so safe and comforting in his arms.

He dropped the towel and took her in his arms. "I love you Candy. I think that I've loved you all my life," Gus said sincerely as he took her into his arms and kissed her. Everything else was forgotten as he lost himself in the fragrance and feeling of this wife of his youth and now, middle years.

As she went into his arms Candace felt something for the first time in years. A slight spark was kindled and she gave herself to him shyly, just as she had on her wedding night so long ago. As he made love to Candace, a sense of obligation and responsibility settled over him.

Although he put his heart and soul into it, for the first time in their thirty years together Gus made love to his wife, but there was no satisfaction achieved by either of them. He was so embarrassed, this had never happened to him before. "I'm sorry baby, I can't tell you how bad I feel. Are you all right? Are you satisfied?"

"It's all right honey, I'm fine. It was probably the drinks you had earlier," Candace made an attempt to soothe him. "We can try again soon," she said as she turned on her side. "Now go to sleep, you'll feel better in the morning.

He could swear that he heard her sigh of relief as he turned on his side. He lay there beside his wife and tried unsuccessfully to empty his mind of that electric moment he'd experienced on that terrace.

Gus felt himself harden and stir as her image hung before his eyes. "What is happening to me?" he wondered as he punched his pillows into shape? "I'm behaving like a sixteen year old football player, one with the *hots* for the cutest cheerleader."

Gus got out of the bed and wandered over to the window overlooking the backyard. "Lord, I thank you for this wonderful life you have so generously given me. Thank you for a lovely wife and two fine sons. For a large family and good friends and for a successful business. You have truly been good to me."

"I ask you to take away these lustful thoughts and wipe that troubling vision from my eyes. Help me to always remember that you joined us together in our youth. Help me to focus all of my attention on the woman in my bed. And please help me identify the cause of her distress. Amen."

He lay back down beside Candace. Gus dozed off and immediately relived the moment on the terrace. He sank down into a deep sleep immediately. For the first time since his military days, he had a very wet dream and restless sleep.

Chapter Two

On Sunday afternoon Carmen checked out of the hotel and drove the short distance to her home. She carefully drove her ten - year - old Mercedes into the garage, picked up her bag, briefcase and laptop and mounted the front stairs of the duplex. She rang the bell and heard an irritable reply from the other side, "why don't you use your keys Carmen, I was watching TV and have to get up."

"Hello to you too, Hugh. Would you please take one of these bags?" She said this as she pushed the door open enough to squeeze through. Hugh was her seventy - year old, retired and tired husband. They had been married for twenty years and retirement had made him no less lazy and dependent than he had been all the years he had worked. He did the minimum cooking and cleaning required to keep her off his back. The majority of his time was spent in front of the TV, asleep or reading and sometimes all three at the same time. His contention was that he had worked hard all his life and all real work of any kind had ceased on the day of his retirement.

To his credit he was a faithful and dedicated worker before he retired. He worked six days a week and overtime each day. He had loved his job and drove to New Jersey in all kinds of weather to take care of Carmen and his inherited family.

Once Hugh retired he did take over most of the housekeeping chores leaving Carmen free to pursue her career and other interests. He also took on her most hated chores, paying the household bills, working diligently to juggle his pension and Carmen's paycheck. His goal was solely to propel them into a debt - free (wishful thinking) middle class existence. He wanted to leave Carmen secure in the event that something (old age/death) happened to him.

Carmen's friend Jessica knew he would need good luck with that. She was working with him to keep Carmen's spending within reasonable limits. She was also identifying investments for them and finding the money to finance same investments. He respected her friend and was more than happy to have the support. Carmen was stubborn and gave him a hard time. She respected Jessica too much to be difficult with her.

He didn't do much driving, shopping or lawn and garden work and he shoveled no snow. However, he redeemed himself by carrying Carmen's packages when she shopped. Hugh also loved to shop and the two of them spent many hours happily shopping in malls and flea markets with her friends. The Salvation Army stores were their favorite haunts. He also loved to cook. Everyone gathered at her house on Sundays to enjoy his peas and rice, curry goat, beef stew and fresh bread.

The only other thing that Hugh was diligent about was sex. He still had a voracious sexual appetite and was always trying to get girlfriend in bed. He acted like he had been on Viagra for years and was not even in line for a heart attack. The problem was his appetite wasn't always backed up with the requisite energy.

Unfortunately for him she was often so worn out emotionally and physically with her job, family and other activities that sex was the farthest thing from her mind.

Occasionally she would be rested enough to play with him. Theirs was a sporadic love life at best. He no longer made a pretense toward being romantic and she couldn't stand the grabbing and groping without the requisite foreplay. There were also other issues Carmen was struggling to resolve within herself in terms of her own personal growth.

Her early life had not been easy and she prayed often for God to grant her and her abuser forgiveness. Sometimes she felt that if she could find one quiet hour in her life, she could examine and resolve every one of those past issues (much of them involved her sexual development). She could then put them to rest once and for all. Then she could also face up to the fact that dark chapter of her life was over and Hugh did not deserve to suffer for the sins of another.

Hugh had no interest in Carmen's job or other activities. He was proud of her in an offhand sort of way. He took her completely for granted, knowing that she would never leave him. She had made him a promise years ago and he believed her.

He had always fussed about the girls and their friends, the telephone and everything else they did or did not do. But only to Carmen. He really loved them dearly. No matter what happened he made sure that he remained their favorite parent.

Their frustrations and anger was always taken out on Carmen. All of their problems were brought to her too. However, he was the one who gave them money and anything else they wanted.

Girlfriend had been listening to a catalog of his complaints every night for the past ten years. Vanessa had not returned home from college; she loved her Dad but could not handle the nagging.

Shawn had recently come back home to have her first baby. Now Hugh had something to nag Carmen about on a daily basis. If it wasn't the baby's illegitimate status, it was Shawn's talking to Luis on the phone every five minutes. He never fussed to Vanessa or Shawn, only Carmen. Now he followed her upstairs, dragging her dress bag and reciting Shawn's sins for the past two days that they were in the house alone.

"I don't know why she talks to that low-life if she doesn't want him. He probably doesn't want to marry her and expects me to take care of his "pickny." You tell him I don't want him coming here. Do you hear me Carmen? You tell him."

"Tell him yourself Hugh. You wear me out with your fussing about the girls. If they upset you; tell them, not me. Did you have dinner?" She changed the subject to divert his attention.

"How was your conference Honey?" She asked herself loudly. "I was fantastic. My boss was so proud of me you would think he was my husband," she answered herself sarcastically.

"What did you say Carmen?" Hugh asked as he aimed the remote control for the bedroom TV. "You know I can't hear you when the TV is on. When are you coming to bed?" He patted her side of the bed as an invitation to join him.

18

"I have to put my things away and get something to eat. I'll be back later." He was busy channel surfing and did not even hear her.

"Mama, I need to talk to you," Shawn called from her room.

"I'm going to fix myself a snack, why don't you come on down and keep me company?" . She prepared a light snack of cheese, crackers and melon, then settled down in the breakfast nook overlooking the backyard. Shawn bounced into the room and hugged her mother tightly from the back.

"Hi pretty Lady. I missed you this weekend."

"Did you really miss me or are you tired of hearing your father fussing?"

"Both Ma, how was your conference?" Shawn was a pretty young , woman. The spitting image of her mother with the same out-going personality and love of life. She had lots of friends. Carmen was disturbed that she could not seem to settle on one young man; until Luis. Even with the baby on the way, Shawn appeared to be distancing herself from him.

Luis was a nice and very responsible young man, anxious to marry Shawn and be a father to their baby. He was Trinidadian with Venezuelan roots. He had the cutest accent and Carmen and Shawn always went into peals of laughter when he tried to say certain things like village and television.

Carmen and Shawn really liked him and suspect-

-ed that Hugh did too: but would never admit it. The two men were baseball nuts and spent hours together; watching Hugh's Yankees even though Luis favored the Mets.

"It was just great. I'm sure to get a bonus from it. The money will come just in time for Grandma to dress her baby. By the way, did you have the sonogram, done, Shawn?

"Oh Ma," she said with shining eyes. "I had my sonogram on Friday and it's a girl, just like you said. I have the picture right here." The two women 'oohed' and 'ahhed' over the picture, turning it this way and that and looking at it from every angle. Truthfully Carmen could not make out her head or foot.

"I guess I'd better get started with her blankets and layette now. She will have to have the works, blankets, sweaters, booties and caps, maybe a quilt too? This is the first baby in the family and your Aunts are going to buy out every piece of baby clothes in the stores. Carmen had four sisters and they all adored Carmen's girls.

I saw the most adorable baby furniture in Macy's and knew it had my baby's name on it. Shawn laughed as her mother forgot all about her and started designing the baby's layette. Her Mama would spend every available moment crocheting for her "new" baby. The "Grandma" would buy every beautifully colored yarn possible and travel everywhere with a bag of varied colored yarn and her ever-present hook.

People would look at her strangely as she picked up a stitch or two at stoplights and every community meeting. But she would dress and wrap her baby in love every single day.

Shawn thought her mother had forgotten to ask the really serious questions. At least she thought she had forgotten until she said, "by the way young lady, we need to talk about your plans. How long do you expect to be able to work? What kind of medical coverage does Luis have? When do you plan to get married? Will the baby be the flower girl at that shindig?

Shawn expected her to produce a questionnaire at any moment. Carmen didn't need it, she knew exactly what to ask. She tried to get an answer in edgewise, but her Mama was on a roll.

"All right Mama, this is not a quiz." Shawn threw up her hands. "Here is the scoop, all of it." The ladies settled down in earnest and began to map out plans for their baby's future.

The first thing on Carmen's list was to get the parents married. "Shawn, we are going to get you and Luis married so that baby will have a legal name. This is my first grandchild and I want the best for her. I don't know why you are being so stubborn, but you'd better come to your senses and soon. Your father is upset and so am I. I've talked to Luis's mother and we are going to take care of everything for you. All you need to do is set a date. That is my final word, I have to go to work now."

Then there was the problem of Vanessa. There had always been sibling rivalry between the sisters. The pregnancy had really brought out the bitchiness in her. Even though "V" was doing well in her career and had been married a year to her Chris, she was obviously upset about her sister's baby.

She was the eldest and felt that it she should present her parents with their first grandchild. Being married herself and stable in her job Vanessa was supposedly embarrassed about her sister's unmarried state and uncertain career. She was driving them all mad with her constant criticisms and negative comments. Carmen knew that Vanessa's problem stemmed not from embarrassment over Shawn's condition. It was jealousy more than anything else.

"V" had done everything right. Graduated from school, landed a responsible job and a good looking, successful husband, but her baby sister was having the first grandchild. She was not happy about that at all."

Monday morning found Carmen at her desk early. She was still excited about the conference and was anxious to hear what her boss had to say. As she sat down at her computer to begin her report, the phone rang.

"Hi Mom, I heard from a big-mouthed, pregnant birdie that your conference went well. Congratulations, you must have turned that place out."

"On a humble tip baby, I have to give God the praise. However, *He/She* sure gave your old Mama the brains and guts to pull this one off. By the way, where were you this weekend?"

"Chris and I spent the weekend in the Pocono's. Mt. Airy Lodge is full of old folks, but it is as beautiful as you said it was. We had a wonderfully restful time."

"We saw a great show and ate lots of good food. You know how much Chris loves his food. He told me to pass on his thanks for the travel tip. I spoke to Dad early this morning and he was fussing about Shawn as usual. What are you going to do about that situation, Mom?"

"I have it in hand, Baby. Shawn and I had a long talk last night. She's just about ready for that wedding. We'll get together later this week. Hopefully, we can start making wedding plans.

Now, let's talk about you. Sweetheart, do you think you finally got pregnant? You know how much your father and I love that place. There's a real possibility that your sister was conceived in one of their heart-shaped Jacuzzi's. Just talking about our trips there brings it all back."

"Mama; you need to remember that I am your daughter and I find it hard to believe that my parents were ever lovers. Let alone moonlight staring, Jacuzzi sharing playmates. However, I will pass this along to Chris. Give him something to aim for. He's got a crush on you as it is. He will really have to go some now to keep up with my Daddy."

The women burst out laughing when Carmen said, "you got that right Number One daughter." Carmen was certain that once the baby came and they all held their precious bundle of joy for the first time, both Hugh and Vanessa would calm down. Meanwhile they were both making her life miserable.

" Oops Baby, I have to go now, Mr. Ames just

came in. Love you Sweetheart."

"Love you Ma, I'll call you later."

"Carmen Ashley, you my dear, are a genius," The portly Mr. Ames gushed. "The conference was all that we had anticipated and more. Congratulations on a job well done. This is the first time our company's projections for the future has been articulated so well."

"Calls are already coming in from new investors so I've been told to offer you my job. Because; thanks to your brilliance I will be moving up to Senior vice president of marketing. Along with your promotion, I personally would like to show my thanks by giving you and Hugh a two-week, all expenses paid vacation to Hawaii. You can take the trip any time you please."

Carmen just stood there and stared at her boss of fifteen years. She finally recovered enough to say; this is incredible and recognition beyond my wildest dreams. There was somewhere else to go in the company, and apparently she'd made it there. She tapped herself lightly on the back of the head. The tap was an unconscious gesture she was in the habit of doing whenever she was nervous, excited or overwhelmed with emotion.

Mr. Ames thought she was undecided so decided to sweeten the pot. "Carmen, I know how much you like this job so if I agree to give you my present salary too, would you accept the promotion?'

"Of course I will accept your offer. Thank you for your confidence Mr. Ames. Thank you for the opportunity to do my job without encumbrance and your ability to overlook the fact that I am a woman."

"A businesswoman Carmen Ashley, that's what you are and a damned good one at that." He said as he shook her hand.

"When do I take over from you Mr. Ames," she asked?

"As soon as you can clear your desk and have your garden moved into my office. Those corner windows should be just the place for your little indoor garden, don't you think?" Mr. Ames strolled out of her office whistling, "Working hard for the money, working hard for the money."

Girlfriend carefully closed her door. Flinging her arms wide she screamed. "Yes, yes, I certainly worked hard, and it sure paid off." For once, she was at a total loss for words. God had just delivered her dream to her wrapped in a smiling portly package.

Carmen was stunned. This was wildest dreams stuff, not reality. She forgot where she was and tapped herself lightly on the back of the head

After she calmed down she picked up the phone and dialed her home. "Hi Hugh," she screamed as quietly as she could. "Guess what happened to your wife ten minutes ago?

"Are you at work Carmen? Someone's Been calling you all morning. I told them to call you there."

"Hugh, did you hear me. I said something imporportant just happened to me."

"Are you at work Carmen? Someone's been calling you all morning and I told them to call you there."

"Hugh, did you hear me? I said something important just happened to me."

"Alright Carmen, I heard you. What happened? Did you get hurt? You know if you fell on the job you should sue them, they can afford to pay you, you know."

"Hugh honey, please listen to me. I got a promotion. I am now junior vice president of marketing. Isn't that great?"

"You should have had that promotion a long time ago," he grumbled. "You are the best thing they've got going and they don't even know it." Hugh was loyal to a fault and believed Carmen capable of just about anything. He simply never listened to her and did not understand anything about her work or any other part of her life.

"Thanks honey, I have to go now. I'll see you later." As she hung up she thought, "what if just once Hugh shared my joy? I wonder if I'd know how to act? I wonder what it would be like to have someone who understood just how difficult it is for a black woman to make it in this man's world. To have someone to wrap me in a teeth-rattling hug, kiss me until I forgot why I was happy in the first place, bought flowers and wine to celebrate. Then fed me at a fancy restaurant. This same someone's kiss would cause me to melt into a puddle of pure, unadulterated need.

He would understands the complexity of my career, and the energy and wit it takes for me to manage it and get ahead. A man who shares my pride in my accomplishments and am as proud of me as I am of myself. Not in an abstracted, taken for granted way, but with genuine sincerity. "Oh well, no sense thinking about something that will never happen."

She pushed the gloomy thoughts aside and sat down at her desk to begin organizing her move into her corner "suite." A large part of Carmen's new duties was dealing with the various private consultants and contractors who provided services to her company. Aramark had the lunchroom concession for all of their buildings, Bell Atlantic provided the communications equipment and Hayden Enterprises provided all of the computers. They were responsible for the installation, maintenance and programming of her firm's two hundred plus computers in several buildings.

In addition to these three large contractors, there was a number of small ones. Mr. Ames gave Carmen a *whole* week to move into her new office, retrain her secretary and familiarize herself with the contents of the various contracts. He then set up a breakfast meeting for the contractors to introduce her as his successor. The meeting was scheduled for two weeks hence. She spent the intervening time reading up on the companies and gathering information on their reps. These were the people she would be working with on a regular basis.

Mr. Ames was helpful up to a point, but Roseatta (his secretary) dished out the real dirt. She gave Carmen detailed descriptions of them all, right down to their salaries and if they picked their noses in public. According to her, several of the men were decent looking and two were downright spectacular. However they were all married, so off limits. Carmen told her facetiously to stop gossiping and went in to work.

On the morning of the meeting Carmen got out of bed early. As she finished dressing and prepared to leave the house, she heard Shawn throwing up in her bathroom. She was a little concerned about such a prolonged bout of morning sickness. Even though she had been plagued by nausea throughout both of her pregnancies. It had eventually passed away. "Are you all right Baby?" she called out.

"No Ma," came the muffled response. "I feel sooo sick."

Carmen pushed open the bathroom door as her daughter lifted her head from the toilet bowl.
Carmen held out her arms and her baby girl came into them gratefully with tears streaming down her face.

"I'm being punished Ma," she cried. I just know it. I'm so sorry Mama. Sorry I got myself into this big old mess. What am I going to do?" Shawn wailed.

"Shh Baby, hush now. You'll make me cry and ruin my make-up." She bathed Shawn's face as she spoke. "I was like this with both of you. I promise the sickness will pass soon and you'll be just fine. Now let's have a hot cup of tea and get your stomach settled. I will drop you off at work. Come on now, you must hurry up because I can't be late this morning.

"Oh Mama, I love you so much. I feel better

already. You go ahead, your meeting is too important for you to be late. I'll be fine. Dad can drop me at the Subway."

I'll see you this evening and we will talk some more. Carmen was convinced that the nausea would go away once Shawn made a decision about the wedding. The excitement alone was probably causing her stomach to be upset. Her own nausea had eventually passed. She hoped Shawn's would after the excitement of the wedding was over.

"Are you sure you are alright Baby?" she called to her."

Shawn came into the hallway and hugged her Mama. Carmen smoothed her baby's hair and kissed the top of her head. Picking up her purse and tote on the way out the door, she called. "I am leaving now Hugh, see you this evening." As she slipped her key in the ignition Carmen thought to herself, I wish he would say goodbye or good luck Baby, just once. It would make all the difference in the world to me. "Oh well", she sighed, If I haven't had a response for the past twenty years, I can forget even looking for one now.

The engine sputtered and caught just before her heart plummeted to her toes. "Thank you Lord, she fervently prayed. I really can't deal with Bessie's foolishness this morning. She made it to the office without mishap and found Mr. Ames's efficient and gossipy secretary Rosetta setting up the conference room.

"Where's Erica? I told her to be here early today." Erica was her own secretary and though she was a great worker, was prone to be too independent and she would pick the oddest times to assert her authority.

"Erica's here Ms. Carmen. She went downstairs to wait for the caterer's delivery truck. Mr. Ames is sure going all out for your introductory meeting with the reps. He said he wants to put some food in their stomachs and mellow them out before he springs you on them."

The two women fell out laughing at Roseatta's joke. Carmen had a reputation in the company for being a ball breaker. She was smart, aggressive and charismatic, therefore threatened people without even being aware of it.

Roseatta and Erica adored and idolized her; Erica emulated her dress so much that sometimes Carmen got the weird feeling that she was looking at a reflection of herself in the mirror. She was enrolled in a local college at night, determined to be the first College graduate in her family too..

Mr. Ames took paternal pride in Carmen's ability and accomplishments and was a constant source of encouragement to her. He gave her full rein of her creativity and watched her work miracles with difficult business problems and personnel. She also worked as hard as any male would have.

Her tension drained away with the laughter and she could feel a healthy burst of adrenalin kick in. I'll be in my office. Please have Erica signal me when it's time to make my entrance." This statement was accompanied by a wink as she firmly closed the door to her private office. She checked her make-up and smoothed the deep red Maggie MacNaughton coatdress down over her ample hips. The dress had a faintly military look due to the black and gold trim. It hit her just below the knees. She hated shoes and stockings but today she wore both. Her three inch, red and black sling back matched her dress. The pumps made her legs look longer and (Thank God) slimmer. The chunky gold earrings, chocker, and bracelet added a slight feminine touch to the severe executive attire.

Unbeknown to her, she made an arresting picture with her perfectly applied and understated make-up. Her pageboy haircut swung gently about her face. The woman's bearing was regal and self-assured and her smile magnetic. Once satisfied with her appearance, she sat down at her desk and became instantly absorbed in her work.

Chapter Three

Gus had a fetish for being on time and was often early for appointments. Jake Ames was an old business contact and personal friend. He had invited him to that "Cocktail Party at the Crowne Plaza" and had asked him to be present at this meeting. Jake had also told his best friend about his promotion to Senior Vice President and that he had selected a woman to take his place.

Jake was not a particularly expressive individual but had *raved* to his friend and colleague about this Mrs. Ashley. Since he trusted his friend's business acumen and character assessments, he was looking forward to meeting this paragon. Establishing a solid working relationship with her would be paramount for his continued success in dealing with their company.

He was so preoccupied with his thoughts, that Jake had to speak to him twice before he heard him. His friend finally clasped him on his shoulder to get his attention. "Hey brother it's good to see you. I was hoping you'd get here early so that I could brief you privately." He then launched into a description of Mrs. Ashley's new role in the company. He explained that even though Gus had not met her personally, he would soon see for himself what a fine executive she was.

Jake wanted to ensure every chance for her success so; he was asking his "Brother and friend" to keep an eye on the group. He was to make sure there were no snide comments or sexist remarks directed toward her. Jake would not take kindly to such behavior and would deal harshly with any perpetrators. Jake also knew that

Carmen would not take kindly to any such remarks either.

Gus gave his promise but idly wondered what Jake was so excited about. His friend was usually so conservative that this woman must really be something special to get him all fired up.

He also idly wondered if his friend could possibly have a *thing* for this Mrs. Ashley. "Nah," he thought to himself. "Jake was much too in love with his third wife. Shannon was a beautiful mulatto, and as much in love with Jake as he was with her.

Jake moved to the head of the table as the room filled up quickly with men and women speculating on the reason for the meeting. His friend called for order and opened the meeting. He began by announcing his promotion and after a few minutes of accepting congratulations, explained that this meeting was not about him but was called to introduce his replacement, Mrs. Carmen Ashley, as he new Senior Vice President of Marketing and Communications.

At that moment Carmen stepped into the room and his life changed forevermore. His mind locked on the face of his dreams and his mind suffered a brief lapse. When he could think again Gus realized why Jake had introduced her as Mrs. Ashley. Even though her business persona was firmly in place; the air moved with an undeniable sexual energy. That was partly due to her dazzling smile and wholly due to the way she moved. He looked around him and watched his colleagues adjust their expressions, so as not to be caught staring.

The woman before them was not classically beautiful but exuded confidence, class and a personality that reached out and enveloped the room. Most of the women and men in this room were openly admiring. However, one woman couldn't hide the jealous expression that flashed across her face. "This should be interesting," Gus thought.

Carmen stepped into the room and stood behind and to the side of Jake Ames. Her eyes began an automatic scan of the room. Suddenly they collided with a familiar set of velvety brown eyes, framed by incredibly beautiful lashes. She had seen those same eyes in her dreams the past two weeks and was totally unprepared for her body's reaction to them.

The air was suddenly sucked out of the room and she momentarily lost her mental balance. Her professionalism kicked in and she immediately tore her eyes away. Carmen continued her scan and as she focused on a warmly smiling female face, heard Jake speaking.

Her heart was beating loudly in her ears and she realized that she had almost lost it. C'mon girl, she chided herself, get a grip. He is just a man, a good-looking stranger that is going to cause you a heart attack. But ultimately, he is just a man. You have a meeting to get through. She shook herself mentally and turned a brilliant smile on Mr. Ames. Could you repeat that last statement, please?" She asked him in a husky voice that went straight to Gus' crotch.

I was simply out-lining your new responsibilities to the ladies and gentlemen Mrs. Ashley. They are all aware that you have taken my place and must now relate to you in all matters pertaining to this company. "Now it is my pleasure to introduce to you formally, Mrs. Carmen Ashley, Senior Vice President of Marketing and Communications.

The room is literally vibrating, Gus thought. I've never seen anyone walk into a room and bring this kind of energy and light. He felt the ground shift and change beneath him. He knew somewhere deep inside that Carmen Ashley would be his *Lady*. Her vibrancy and energy, her incredible sexiness and the voice that raised the hairs on his arms; all of the woman and everything that made her, would be absorbed into his being.

He realized that he had saved himself for her with -out knowing it and he was glad. "This must be what the *Older Brothers* had been teasing him about." They (*the brothers*) were amazed that he had been married to the same woman for nearly forty years and fathered only his three *"Yard"* children (none outside the home).

Their theory was that he was getting ready to hit middle age and a crisis was eminent. They probably were laying bets on the timing. With that thought he relaxed in his chair, crossed his legs and began to pay attention to his *Lady's* presentation. He was not amazed at the way she held that room spell bound: She had mesmerized him in a few seconds flat.

Her voice was as deep as his own, as she asked the group to introduce themselves. Several male voices spoke up at once, vying for her attention. She flashed a dazzling smile and said; "Ladies and Gentlemen, we have plenty of time. Today we are here to get acquainted and establish some basic ground rules.

Let's start with the gentleman to my left, your name sir," She said as she pointed to a man to her left. "Wesley Owens here," a deep voice boomed out.

"Showtime girlfriend," she said to herself. "Wesley Owens, you are our representative from Bell Atlantic and you supervise all of our communications installations. Am I correct, Sir"

"Indeed you are Madam, pleased to make you acquaintance.'

"Likewise Mr. Owens," she said and continued around the room in the same manner. She put the group at ease while impressing them with her knowledge of their company's role in connection with her own. She also impressed them with her style and grace. As she came to Gus, he spoke up.

"Augustus Hayden here ma'am. I am the president and CEO of Hayden Enterprises. I have heard a great deal about you, Mrs. Ashley. I'm looking forward to our association." His message to her was clear. They would be friends and more, it was inevitable.

"So am I Mr. Hayden, I can assure you that we will work well together. "Thank you sir," was her *verbal* reply. "I heard you and believe you, was her *non-verbal* reply to him. To herself she thought, "I'd like to work with him in more ways than one. Too bad we are both married. Augustus Hayden could easily make a woman forget her vows and that's for sure."

"I am surely going mad," Gus thought to himself. A smile from that lady makes me feel like I've been worked over by a bull, but is still sitting in a dusty arena. waiting for it to come back and finish me off. I think I like the feeling." He laughed inwardly at himself.

Carmen saw his grin and bristled. "Could our Mr. Hayden be laughing at me? Oh well girlfriend, you'd better laugh too and remember that you are both married. This relationship had better be established as business and kept on a strictly professional footing."

The meeting adjourned without further emotional upheaval on either side and Mr. Ames complimented Carmen on her successful handling of the reps. "Those reps are the best their companies have to offer. They are already eating out of your hand and will give you the best of their service. For example; Gus Hayden, I addition to being president of his company, is one of the best systems analysts in the business. He is honest and efficient; he also has more integrity than anyone that I know of. By the way Gus is also my Lodge brother. I know you will enjoy working with him. I told him all about you and he will have your back just as he's had mine over the years."

"Thank you Mr. Ames, for your confidence and protection," she said only half facetiously. Foregoing their usual handshake she hugged him tightly. Carmen was an emotional woman; she valued Jake Ames and was humbled by his faith in her. She considered him as much more than a business colleague or her boss. Saucily giving him a high five, she left for her office and the mountain of paperwork her new position entailed. This position would be a challenge, but she was confident that she would be up to it.

She wasn't so sure about the drama at home. Dealing with Shawn, a wedding and an imminent birth was something else again.

Jake walked his friend to the elevator and asked him; "what do you think of my new VP? Is she everything I told you she was?"

Gus shook his head and replied; "she had us all eating out of her hands. I sense a real toughness beneath that classy and feminine veneer."

'"You are right about that my Brother. Carmen is brilliant and tough but she also has a heart. I know you are going to like her and enjoy working with her."

"You are right on all counts, Jake. She's going to help me take this business to a new level this year."

Chapter Three

Several weeks later Carmen had worked later than usual. She was the last one to leave the building. She crossed the parking lot and got into the Mercedes. Of course the engine refused to turn over. After several attempts and much praying and coaxing, she decided to call Hugh and ask him to come for her. As she was digging in her purse for her cell phone, a male voice inquired, "May I be of assistance, Mrs. Ashley"

Gus and his grandsons had been on their way from a Soccer game. As he passed the parking lot, he saw a familiar figure standing by an obviously disabled Mercedes Benz. The hood was up and the parking lot was deserted. An alarming scene (or so Gus thought). He figured that he should check to see if she was alright. Jake would have his head if he did nothing and something bad happened to his rising star.

"Good evening, Mr. Hayden, thank God you stopped. I can't seem to get this thing started."

"Let me give it a try, maybe it will start for me." He turned the key in the ignition and got no response. He then opened the bonnet and looked at the spark plugs. They looked dirty but it might have been the light. He lifted up the breather cap on the carburetor . He told her to get in and start the car on his signal.

The engine turned over on the first try and she said a quick prayer of thanksgiving. "Mr. Hayden, I can't thank you enough, you came along just as I was getting a bit nervous."

You should have this car serviced immediately, Mrs. Ashley,' Gus said sternly. "This parking lot is not safe at night and some thug could have stopped with mayhem in mind; and please call me Gus. I feel that we are friends now that I have rescued you from some unknown danger."

"You just *may have* rescued me Gus." She put out her hand and said hesitantly, "My name is Carmen. I'm sorry but I have to go now. My husband must be wondering where I am this late."

"I will follow you home in case the car cuts off again." She started to open her mouth but he held up his hand. "Don't even bother to protest Ma'am. Just get in and start the car."

"Thank you Mr. Hayden, uh Gus. I really appreciate this."

"It is no problem Ma'am. I am right behind you."

"Gus climbed into the Expedition and followed the old Mercedes down the highway.

"Who is the pretty Lady Grandpa?" Little Gus asked?

"A business acquaintance son," he answered the little boy as he watched Carmen's taillights up ahead.

"Why did you stop and help her Grandpa?" asked Jon, Jr.

"I helped her because gentlemen always help

ladies when they are in trouble boys, remember that."

Carmen pulled into the driveway next to the duplex and blew her horn. Gus drove past, tooted his horn in reply and he and boys waved. They headed for the Brooklyn-Queens Expressway and home.

The next few weeks flew by for Carmen. She adjusted well to her new role and began looking forward to her granddaughters' arrival. She was crocheting a layette so always had her yarn and hook close by. Shawn's nausea had finally gone away and she sparkled and bloomed with good health.

The only problem looming in the background was Shawn's indecision regarding marriage to Luis. The boy was driving her crazy trying to get her to use her influence on her daughter.

For once Carmen agreed with Hugh that It was past time Shawn made a decision one way or the other. Neither of them wanted the preacher to perform the ceremony during labor or after the child turned twenty. However, the decision was Shawn's and only Shawn's. She tried to get Hugh as well as Luis to understand that fact. They all just had to be patient with Shawn and hope she'd make the right decision.

Hugh fussed all of the time because she hadn't made up her mind about Luis and was insisting to have this baby out of wedlock. He said he wasn't going to raise any little bastards. She tried to calm him down with vague explanations of emotional upheavals brought on by pregnancy and immaturity. She told all of them that

Shawn would change with motherhood. Secretly, she too was out of patience with the little mother, so she wasn't really all that convincing.

Then there was the problem of Vanessa. There had always been sibling rivalry between the sisters. The pregnancy had really brought out the bitchiness in her. Even though "V" was doing well in her career and married for over a year. She was embarrassed about her sister's unmarried state and uncertain career. She was adding to the confusion with her constant criticisms and negative remarks.

Carmen prayed everyday that once the baby came, and they held their precious bundle of joy for the first time. Both Hugh and Vanessa would calm down. Meanwhile they were making her life miserable.

Late one afternoon as she was clearing up her desk in preparation to leave for the day. The phone rang, Carmen answered; "Good afternoon, Carmen Ashley speaking."

"Good afternoon Mrs. Ashley, Carmen?" a deep familiar voice responded. "Something has come up that I think you should be made aware of I believe we need to discuss it. The situation is rather urgent. May I come over now?"

She hesitated briefly. Tonight was her monthly political club meeting and she had planned to rush home and make dinner for Hugh. However if the matter was this urgent, what could she do? She had to meet with him soon and it might as well be now. "I was planning to leave soon Gus, are you nearby?"

"I can be there in ten minutes. By the way. By the way, thank you Carmen Ashley." Gus hung up his mobile phone. As he pulled the Expedition out into traffic, he wondered why the hesitation? I certainly don't want to inconvenience her, but the glitches in her communications software need to be straightened out immediately.

If the two of them decided to work together the problem would be solved in a matter of minutes and they both would be on their way to their respective homes."

She ushered Gus into her office. "Mr. Hayden, uh Gus, I hope I didn't sound ungracious when you called, but I have a meeting at seven and for once I was planning a home-cooked meal for my family."

"I am truly sorry to inconvenience you, Ma'am, but this problem needs our immediate attention. It shouldn't take long to outline." He then began to explain the problem in detail. It centered on the Computerized Voice Messaging Center. It appeared that the upper level executives simply did not know how to access and use the system properly.

Their fumbled attempts caused other units to malfunction, or deactivated already installed units. He suggested coming in and giving classes. Since many of the high-level company executives needed the training, he suggested individualized training also.

The classes would require two trainers and a clerical worker to set up the appointments. Gus and the other technician would individually guide each staff member through the set-up and use of their phone system. Carmen offered the use of her Conference Room and they agreed on a start date They shook hands and although a minor shook them both, they ignored the contact and parted company.

"I hope he didn't feel that," she thought to herself.

Gus was in and out of her office almost daily during the next three months. At first they spoke politely about business matters. As time passed the conversations became more personal. They were always careful not to touch each other, but looked forward to spending time together.

Gus in particular enjoyed the time spent in her office. She was efficient, independent and an excellent communicator. He was impressed with the way she operated, balancing the tightrope of professional woman executive against her obvious feminity.

She was in constant motion and was often engaged in two other activities while conversing with him. He had never been with anyone whose energy level matched his own. She was curious about everything she saw or heard.

Once she found out that he was a member of a Masonic lodge, she pumped him for information about their rites an d rituals. He teasingly invited her to join and spoke to her about the Order of the Eastern Star. He was Patron of a chapter of "Sisters" and always interested in recruiting members.

Carmen listed all of her other activities for him

and told him that as nosy as she was, there was simply no time in her schedule for another activity. Besides with her first grandchild's imminent arrival, every extra minute would be focused on her.

He was intelligent, a great conversationalist and a good listener. He was also funny in a dry and obscure way. He loved to tell corny, slightly risqué jokes that he downloaded from his e-mail. Although she received many of them too, she still found them funny and laughed her head off. But it was his dry straight-faced delivery that delighted her the most.

Gus could tell a joke with a completely dead face. She would crack up and he would look at her and ask, "what's so funny?" His expression would not have changed.

They talked about everything under the sun. Sharing confidences and secrets. She knew that he had to care a great deal for her and trust her, to open up and share as much of himself as he did in those hours.

Her shower stall was her confessional. She acknowledged there, that she was in love with him. There would never be a romantic liaison, not even the occasional stolen moments. The time they shared in her office was it. All they would ever have. They were married to other people and the price of their love would come too high.

She told him all about her family and confided her concern for Shawn. The baby was due next month and she still had made no decision about marriage. Luis was driving them all crazy. His family was staunchly

Catholic and they were afraid the baby wouldn't be allowed to be christened in Church if they weren't married. Hugh agreed with him and was giving her an exceptionally hard time. The two of the were driving Carmen crazy trying to get her to use her influence on her daughter.

She had run out of patience and finally agreed with Hugh that it was past time Shawn made a decision one way or the other, neither of them wanted the preacher to have to perform the ceremony during labor or after the child turned twenty. Even more disturbing would be a wedding ceremony and christening at the same time.

However the decision was Shawn's and only Shawn's. She tried to get herself and Hugh, as well as Vanessa and Luis to understand that fact. They all just had to be patient with Ms. Preggy and hope she'd make the right decision, and soon.

Hugh fussed all of the time because she hadn't made up her mind about Luis and was insisting to have this baby out of wedlock , and said he wasn't going to raise any little bastards. She tried to calm him down with vague explanations of emotional upheavals brought on by pregnancy and immaturity. She eventually told all of them to just pray. Shawn would change with motherhood. She hoped that she was convincing.

He sympathized with Carmen and told her outrageous anecdotes to take her mind off her problems. He appreciated her laughter even though he realized that his jokes weren't all that funny. He repaid her kindness by really listening to her and encouraged her to find some personal space for herself. Her career was in fine shape but her personal life was totally out of sync. Gus believed that until the two worlds harmonized, his new friend would be continually tied in knots. Privately he realized that she desperately needed someone to talk to, not necessarily asking for advice, but as a sounding Board. He intended to be just that.

Gus was easy to talk to and she often wondered why Hugh no longer wanted to talk or even listen to her. In her innermost secret self, she admitted that they had never really talked. Conversation had fallen by the same wayside as their love life. At one time it was fairly decent but mostly initiated by her. Hugh was an unimaginative lover. He didn't require much I the way of stimulation.

She had taught him enough to get by, but he didn't have a romantic bone in his (fairly handsome and well-kept) body. She had long tired of trying to find non-ego threatening ways to "stroke his male ego" and to teach him simple tricks to stimulate her.

She required a great deal of stimulation of both her mind and body. Unfortunately, she had long resigned herself to the fact that her buttons would never all be pushed. That the romance of her Arabesque, Zebra, Silhouette and beloved Danielle Steele would pass her right on by.

Hugh had always fancied himself as something of a stud (being of Caribbean descent) and drove her nuts wanting to make love anytime he thought about it. For years Carmen put up with his voracious? appetite to keep the peace. In the past few years she tired of the pretense.

The past few years found it more difficult to pretend. Her sister put it down to the change of life. Carmen was honest enough with herself to admit that she was bored out of her mind. She needed her tubes completely blown out at least once or twice before she gave up the ghost to middle-age sterility. She never expected that it would happen until Gus and his long-lashed bedroom eyes, hairy muscular arms and deep, sexy hairy chest blew into her life.

She was always restless and unsettled when she left Gus. She often found her thoughts straying to him in times of stress. And after a few weeks of close proximity found herself dreaming steamy, passionate dreams filled with images of the two of them engaged in passionate, impossibly fulfilling lovemaking. She was so restless at times that she left her bed and spent the night at her computer.

There she played out her fantasies by writing a romance novel. She used her fantasies of Gus to weave a magical, erotic tale of love and romance. She wrote each night until she tired herself out enough to sleep. Sometimes she would put Isaac Hayes in the CD player and listen to him sing; "If Loving You Is Wrong" or Erica Baddoo sing "Secret Lover" until she wore herself out enough to go to sleep.

Hugh has always fancied himself as something of a stud (being of Caribbean origin) and drove her crazy wanting to make love any time he thought about it. For years Carmen put up with his voracious appetite to keep the peace, the appetite was there but the meal was not satisfying for her. In the past few years she tired of the pretense.

Her sister put it down to the change of life; Carmen was honest enough with herself to know that she was bored out her mind and needed her tubes completely blown out at least once or twice before she gave up the ghost to middle-age sterility.

She never expected that it could or ever would happen until Gus and his long lashed bedroom eyes, hairy muscular arms and deep sexy chest blew into her life. Even married women were entitled to day dream.

She was always restless and unsettled when she left Gus and found her thoughts straying to him often in times of stress, she also dreamed steamy, passionate dreams filled with images of the two of them engaged in passionate, impossibly fulfilling lovemaking.

She was so restless at times she got up and spent the night at the computer where she played out her fantasies by starting to write a romance novel. She used her fantasies of Gus to weave a magical, erotic tale of love and romance. She wrote each night until she tired herself out enough to sleep. She would put Isaac Hayes in the CD player and listen to him sing; "If Loving You Is Wrong" or Erica Baddoo sing "Secret Lover" until she wore herself out enough to go to sleep.

Chapter Four

Gus was not doing any better. He had plenty of problems to occupy him. He was working with Carmen and her staff to solve the communications problems at her company. They were slowly getting the executives trained (even Jake had sat still for a session or two), and was satisfied with the progress. They made an excellent team. They were efficient and focused and their trainees rewarded them by learning the system and some even ask -ed for an advanced computer lab.

Gus was an excellent teacher and his staff worked well with hers. They both felt that they were making real progress and agreed with their trainees that further train- ing in basic computer technology might be helpful to the employees and the solution to the problem.

On his home front, Candace appeared to be se- verely depressed. No amount of coaxing could get her to open up and share her problems with him. He had brought her flowers and gifts to cheer her up. She would thank him with a sad smile that really alarmed him. She went to work every day and he asked if there were any problems there. She answered in the affirmative, She had been a staff nurse at Kings County Hospital for twenty years. She loved her job and had many friends on the staff. Obviously that was not the source of her prob- lem. She only brightened up when her grandsons and their god daughter Courtney spent time at the house.

He wondered briefly if Candace could on some primitive level of consciousness know that he was devel- oping an interest in another woman. After the failed

attempt at making love to her the night he had met Carmen, they had made indifferent love several times. Neither of them was passionately interested in sex, but thirty
years of habit is kind of hard to break. Expectations often exceed the will or inclination to act.

Courtney adored Gus, as did all the children in
their circle. She still brought all of her problems to him
even though she was a lovely and vibrant fifteen -year
old. "God poppa can I speak to you in private." She had
asked him a few days ago. "Of course Courtney love.
What's your problem this time? Are the boys still teasing
you about your braids?"

"God Poppa, don't tease me now. I have a serious
problem. Please help me, please, please."

"Of course I will Munchkin," he told the teenager. Come , let's go into my office and get comfortable." Courtney shocked Gus with the information that
she had found in the back of her Mama's closet when she
was looking for an old dress to use as a Halloween cos-
tume.
The child had found her birth certificate and
adoption papers. They were packed in a tote bag along
with her infant blanket and hospital bracelet. Her *Mama
Linda* had never even told her that she was adopted. The
child was devastated. She had tried to speak to her godmother, but Candace just burst into tears. The child had
ended up comforting her. Now she was afraid of hurting
her Mama Linda by asking any more questions.

Gus held the child and comforted her and promised to do what he could. He assured her that they all lov
-ed her and tat she certainly belonged to them.

To himself he resolved to get to the bottom of the matter as soon as possible. He decided to call his friend Troy. His brother was also an attorney. He should be able to help Gus with this or at least give him some legal advice.

He sent Courtney home for the papers and called Troy. His *Brother* was the family attorney. According to what the papers revealed, he was much more. "Hey man, Gus here. I need to set up an appointment with you as soon as possible and I have something I want you to see."

"How about right now. I will always make time for you Bro.

" I'll be right over." Gus said and hung up. He called out to his wife upstairs, "Candy, I'm going over to Troy's I'll be back soon."

There was no reply so he assumed she was upstairs, in fact she was in their bathroom throwing up.

Troy greeted his friend and brother at the door. "What's up Man? You look like mighty serious. Gus just handed the manila envelope stamped with the address of his law office. "Do you need to open that before we open this conversation? I did and I have no idea what to say about the contents of that envelope.

Troy looked at his friend with eyes filled with guilt and pain. "I have known for years that this day was bound to come. I have rehearsed this scene over and over in my head for the past fifteen years. I could not bring myself to say the words that is sure to end our relationship. You are the best friend that a man could ever have. I am going to ask you to keep our fishing date on Saturday. We can talk while the boys are fishing. It will be quiet on Montauk Point and we will be able to talk without distractions."

Gus told his best friend and lodge brother that until yesterday he had no idea that there was a situation. But they could defer their conversation until Saturday. Gus put the whole mess out of his mind for the rest of the week. On Saturday the men took Gus's grandson's fishing on Long Island. Jon, Jr. took his little brother to play among the sand dunes and the men settled down in the back of the Expedition to talk.

"Are you ready to tell me just exactly what happened while I was in Iraq?" Gus asked his friend.

"When you left to go on assignment you asked me to take care of both homes. Candace was working and the boys were in school. I was in and out of your house on practically a daily basis. Candace really missed you. Not just to talk to, but to change light bulbs, keep the boys in line, service the car and whatever else needed to be done around the house. You know me well enough to know that I really looked after all of them. One night the boys had gone to bed. We were sitting in the kitchen having a drink.

She started to cry and I took her in my arms and held her. One thing led to another and we ended up in bed. My feelings were totally mixed. Elation that I finally had the woman I had loved since we were in High School in bed, disloyalty to my wife and betrayal of my best friend. That was the one and only time we made love. Two months later Candace called me over one evening. She was hysterical and in tears. She told me that she was pregnant There was no doubt that the child was mine. She wanted to tell you the truth, but knew she couldn't do it while you were in combat. She would not consider abortion and would only consider adoption to someone she knew.

I suggested asking my wife Mavis. You know that I have always wanted kids. Mavis could not conceive and I had already accepted the fact that I would never have any children. I had always been open to adoption but Mavis refused to think of taking care of any child not her own. Of course we didn't tell her the child was mine. Nor did we mention that the mother was Candace. She turned me down flat anyway.

Linda stepped in at that point and offered to take the baby. It was a closely guarded secret in our circle that Linda was a lesbian. This would stop all the speculation about her. Also Candace and Linda looked so much alike, there would never be any questions asked (even in the family).

Candace and Linda went to California for the last three months of the pregnancy. Remember that Candace wrote you that she and Linda had to spend a few months with their parents? Mavis and I kept your boys. Candace did not want to take them out of school.

The baby would be born in California. Everything went as planned. I flew out there for the birth, and to take care of all the legal work. The sisters brought Courtney home when she was six weeks old. I am pretty sure you know that I have been in love with Candace

Being the family attorney it was natural that I took care of everything for the ladies. You weren't here so I was able to be her "godfather" those first years. Being a father was a brand new experience and one I treasured. You were on special assignment with the Reserves when Courtney was born. She naturally accepted me as her Godfather, until you came home.

"Okay, but even though I was gone for a year, she's had fifteen years to tell me."

"I can't tell you what to do, I can only tell you this whole thing has been hard on your wife and sister-in-law. Candace didn't want to tell you but she can't lie to you either."

"She's been trying to find the right time to tell you and Courtney and it just never came. She is also afraid that Courtney is going to really look at those papers and see who her birth parents are. Linda is afraid that Courtney will think that we didn't want her. However the child is told or whoever tells her, will cause even more confusion.

She loves Linda and knows clearly that she is her mother. But once it is out in the open, the resemblance between Candace and Courtney will be more obvious. They even have the same identical expressions.

"We adults will have to find a solution that the child can handle. We are also going to have to do some serious praying. God will give us the strength to sort this out. We are human and prone to sin. He however, is in the forgiveness business. My first priority is Candace and her mental state. I assume you are willing to take financial and moral responsibility for your daughter. I will talk to my godchild and try and help her get some kind of perspective that so that she can go on with her life. She young and resilient, she'll sort it out eventually. We jus have to be there for her. By the way, Courtney is your legal heir. Where does she fit in the legal wrangling that's going on with you and Mavis?

"She is well provided for. I set up a trust fund for her when she was born. She is my only child and will be entitled to my whole estate. Besides Mavis wanted nothing from me. She walked out with her jewelry and he clothes on her back. Her Daddy and brothers will see that she has everything that she wants or needs. She even left her car.

I'm going to check on my Godsons before they get into mischief, want to come along?"

"No man, I'll stay here. I have some thinking to do. Sitting here by the ocean is the best place for it." Gus sat there and let the salt air wash over him. He closed his eyes and a vision of Candace hung there. Her eyes sad with such an expression of misery etched upon her features, that his heart clenched for her. I wonder when I will stop thinking of her as a child.

All the same I have always loved her. She was my youth and my future all rolled into one. We had such joyous times together, growing up and raising our children. Where did all the love go? When did I lose the passion?

I am not an old man. Why just a few years ago, my Jones got hard just thinking of my beautiful wife. Now we can both be stark naked in a Jacuzzi and I don't

want her nor she me. I hope my growing feelings for
Carmen is not taking away thirty years of loving and car-
ing.

I tell you Lord, he said as he raised his eyes up-
ward. I am just a man, with a man's feelings and needs.
I cannot hope to know how any other man could be feeling in this situation, but I can certainly empathize with a
man caught between his head, heart and Jones. I wonder
if every man at some time, has not come face to face
with himself, his most primal urges and doing the right
thing.

The President of this country lost the battle, as
have kings, cardinals, judges and other high officials. I
guess it all comes down to the fact that you made us
"Man" with all the attendant passion and equipment to
use it. I am fighting this battle and I am going to go a
step further and remove myself from the field for a
while. Maybe when I get back home, some of these
problems will have worked themselves out.

While Troy took the boys for a walk on the
beach. Gus settled down with a beer and his thoughts.
By the time Troy brought them back they were worn out
and hungry. The men gathered the little boys and headed
for McDonald's and home.

As Gus drove from Montauk Point to East Flatbush, he thought about the things he and Troy had talked
about. He knew that he should be angry with him. But
how could he, knowing how he felt about Carmen. He
did not want to lose a lifetime friendship and excellent
business relationship over this. This was definitely time
to put his Christian principles to work.

Carmen decided on the spur of the moment to use her tickets to Hawaii and affect a two-week getaway for her and Hugh. They could be back before the baby's arrival on the scene. She called Gayle her travel agent, and asked her to book her a flight and seven days on Waikiki Beach.

She even decided to splurge and rent a car. She had been to Honolulu before and missed a lot of the sights. With a car she didn't have to depend on the formal tours, they could meander around the island at will; even take a small plane and island hop.

She asked Vanessa to keep an eye on her sister . She promised Luis he would die if he didn't leave Shawn alone about getting married. She told Hugh to get his things out so she could pack for them and prepared to go. Hugh didn't act happy about the trip but Carmen knew he loved to travel. Once he got to the airport and had a couple of Mai Tai's under his belt, he would be fine.

She cleaned off her desk Friday and left early. "Erica tell Mr. Hayden they can continue to use the conference room in my absence and I will see him when I get back." Mr. Hayden called this morning," Erica said. "He's also going to be out of town and that cute Adam will be running things for him. I'll be certain to accommodate him." She laughed at the expression on Carmen's face.
"Just teasing Mrs. Ashley, just teasing," Erica laughed.

Carmen and Hugh left J.F.K. on Saturday morning and after a three-hour layover at O'Hare in Chicago they headed west, toward the Pacific Ocean and Hawaii.

Hugh had a few drinks and went to sleep, but Carmen made friends with the young couple sitting beside them and they watched the movie and talked until they fell asleep. They arrived at Honolulu International Airport around four in the afternoon.

The airport looked like a tropical garden, and smelled delicious. Certainly unlike the impersonal bustle of JFK International. Carmen had been to Jamaica a few times and the Bahamas, and the heat and humidity enveloped you as you disembarked the plane. A balmy breeze greeted them as they disembarked the plane.

The airport looked more like the atrium lobby of a hotel than an airport and the air carried a tangy, fresh and fragrant breeze. The hotel had a tour bus waiting for them complete with Wahini's and leis' for the guests.

Hugh was finally relaxing and Carmen felt good just being away from home. The trip from the airport was interesting. The driver gave a running commentary of the sights on the way and told us of "must see places" to visit while on Waikiki.

Lou and Angela, my new friends, were there for a Union Convention and invited us to hang out with them at their Local's reception. Carmen appreciated the invitation, but told them she expected to spend a lot of time taking in the spectacular views and watching the sights and sounds of Honolulu.

Their room was lovely with two double beds, a huge TV and their own refrigerator and coffee maker. After unpacking, Hugh took a nap and Carmen's first shopping trip was to the ABC store to stock up on supplies. Rim and snacks for Hugh, coffee and Bailey's for her.

She planned to spend a lot of time on the terrace soaking up the unobstructed view of Diamond Head Crater, the ocean, the mountains and crocheting the baby's layette. She also expected to get in periodic naps. As she stepped onto the Lanai she felt sleepy. She sank down onto a deck chair and turned her face to the sun. Oh yes, she thought, life cannot get any better than this.

Within the next few days, Carmen drove Hugh from one end of Waikiki to the other. They spent a whole day at the International Market Place and Kapiolani Park off Kalakaua Avenue. They took the trolley car to Aloha Stadium on Wednesday for the Flea Market, where they bought souvenirs for everyone.

On Thursday they joined Angela and Lou at the new Convention Center, where they saw Rev. Jessie Jackson address thousands of Union members. They got so carried away with the union spirit that they joined in a demonstration to aid the Hawaiian government workers in their bid for a long awaited pay raise.

By Friday Hugh was tired of sightseeing and hanging out with their new friends. He had discovered the large screen TV in the bar and it was always tuned in to some sports event from the Mainland, usually the Yankees. They also served excellent Jamaican rum that, of course, Hugh was partial to. He refused to budge when Carmen headed to the beach and was on the same stool when she came back through an hour later drenched.

The surf was deceptively high and she misjudged

the height of the waves. She had bent over to pick up a bikini she saw floating by and a wave crashed over her, knocking her down and washing her own bag out to sea.

Carmen was so disgusted with herself that she left the beach fussing that she would never go back. Hugh did not even look up as she told him, "Come up in an hour. We have to get dressed for dinner."

She spent Saturday morning lazing around the room and sunning on the terrace. In the afternoon she went downstairs to the Beauty Salon and pampered herself with a manicure, pedicure and new hair do.

The Sheraton sat right next to a mall with the most delicious shops so she used her American Express card to advantage and bought herself a hot, red jersey cocktail shift with spaghetti straps and a cleverly draped bodice. She was determined that Hugh notice her tonight at dinner.

They had dinner in the Top of Waikiki, a revolving restaurant at the top of the business plaza. The view of Diamond Head and Waikiki was spectacular and the food delicious. They had both dined on delicious seafood dishes and had their favorite drinks as they watched the show. They (Carmen and Hugh) made a handsome couple and since the Mai Tai's were excellent, he was in a mellow mood.

They enjoyed the Hawaiian revue and sang the Hawaiian Wedding song along with everyone else. Carmen was into her Bailey's and made up her mind that if Hugh's good mood continued and if he could dredge up some romance, she too was long overdue for a night of lovemaking. Hawaii truly lives up to its hype. And maybe it would work it's magic on Hugh.

They were both a little high as they finished their last drink. Carmen loved this vacation thing. She was not a real drinker, but she did love her Bailey's, Mudslides and Pina Colada's. Now she added Mai Tai's to her meager list. It was great not having to worry about being the designated driver. She gathered their things and prepared to leave the restaurant as Hugh paid the check and tipped the lovely waitress lavishly.

As they waited for the elevator that would take them to the Lobby, she asked Hugh. "Are you enjoying yourself Hugh? Hawaii truly lives up to it's hype. I'm so glad we got a chance to get away before the baby makes her appearance."

" That Luis is driving me crazy. She's on the phone every minute she's home talking to him or complaining about him.. She cries at the drop of a hat and embarrasses me with my friends, calling me Grandpa and knowing she ain't even married. In my day a fellow knocked a girl up, he had to marry her, point blank and no discussion and all feelings about it aside. Maybe I should just get out my shot gun and take them over to your preacher friend," he fumed.

"Oh hell," Carmen swore to herself. "This man just can't keep a mood going. Here we are in a sexy glass bubble, floating through space, enveloped by a breathtaking view of the ocean, with a backdrop of stars and sky.

I am half high and more amorous than I have .

been in years. I'm wearing a non-dress that begs for some risque behavior and what do I get? I get one of the "grumpy old men" too dim to take advantage of his woman. He doesn't even realize that I only need a nudge in the direction of the nearest bed to make his dreams come true.

All he can do is o on about some grown young'uns two thousand miles away. They are probably doing right now what we ought to be doing. By the time the elevator doors opened, Carmen's mood was truly blown.

"Carmen I was talking to you. You never listen to me. I need to go back to the bar. I want to check on the Yankees, they probably won and I don't even know the score."

She said something extremely uncomplimentary about the Bronx Bombers under her breath. To Hugh she said sweetly, You go on ahead Honey. I'm going upstairs to jump off the terrace naked, okay."

"Alright Carmen, you go on ahead and do what you want. I'll see you later."

Sarcasm is totally lost on that man, she fumed. I might as well go upstairs, have a drink and write in my diary. Or, better yet plan our schedule for next week. I have so many things left on my "must do list" and time is running out. She kicked off her shoes, regretfully shim-mied out of that hot-for-nothing dress and poured herself A healthy shot of Bailey's Irish Cream. She turned on one of favorite Sam Cooke tapes and settled at the table on the Lanai with her electronic planner and the pamphlets, brochures and flyers gathered for her by her friends Mary Grace and Carlotta.

She decided start the week with the famous Germaine's Luau. Hugh should like that. This was supposed to be the most authentic Luau. There was a show, lots of food and drinks in a natural, primitive setting. As long as there was lots of food, half-naked women and music, Hugh was fine. Her husband ought to feel right at home, she thought facetiously.

She set aside Tuesday for a stroll down Ala Mauna Boulevard with stops at the Arsenal, the statue of King Kamehameha, the Library and the Government Complex. The evening would be devoted to dinner on a yacht at sea. Wednesday was Diamond Head day and a visit to some of the authentic Hawaiian neighborhoods. She made a note to engage a tourist guide for that eclectic blend of cultures.

She felt that her native Brooklyn must be much the same. She was truly in love with this beautiful island. She also planned to shop for some authentic native fabric. She wanted to make a lounge dress and some sofa cushions for herself.

Her most exciting trip she planned for Thursday. Carmen had wanted to visit Pearl Harbor and the Arizona Memorial since she was a small child. She was born in 1944. Somehow she felt that she was a war baby or at least she was born in the aftermath of the big war. Her Mama told them stories of the difficult years and had even preserved some of their family's ration and gas stamps. Her Mama's sister (Maj. Janie Jenkins) and her favorite aunt as well as a couple of uncles had been in the Military. Her Aunt Janie had mustered out at Ft. DeRussey. She idolized her Aunt and felt that a visit to the Fort would bring her even closer. One of her fathers brothers (Vardry Fleming, Jr.) was in the navy. A picture of him had hung in their living room when she was a child.

By the time Hugh came in she was poring over the brochure for the Polynesian Cultural Center. Mary Grace had told her to dress comfortably and wear sneakers. She knew Carmen would want to see everything and stuff herself on the gourmet feast. She had her back pack and plenty of film already prepared. "Hugh are you going with me tomorrow?"

"Carmen you are wearing me out. You forget I'm on vacation. I am retired and you're making this into another job. Go ahead and do what you want. I think I'm sticking close to the hotel from now on."

Not on your life Mister. I paid good money for some of these trips and we are going together." Hugh mumbled something too low for her to hear and turned his back to the door. A few minutes later she heard him snoring lightly. She picked up her diary and began to re-arrange her schedule. She planned to give him a few days to enjoy himself. She knew that he would miss her by the end of the week. They still had time to do some things together. What an utter waste of lovely moonlight and good music.

Early Monday morning Carmen rearranged her schedule. She moved the trip for the Cultural Center to Monday, the Yacht trip to Tuesday and Luau to Friday. The woman at the Tour Desk was totally frustrated by seven am when Carmen completed her arrangements to her satisfaction, and collected her tickets.

She set out for the Cultural Center while Hugh was still asleep and met her friend Rikki on the bus. They were both inveterate tourists and liked the same things. By the time they disembarked the bus, they had agreed to spend the day together.

The Center was everything and more that the women expected as they toured the different Islands, rode down the river in a canoe with a handsome Hawaiian at the helm. They watched the Polynesian Odyssey in the Imax Theater and the Royal Barge Spectacle on the River. Carmen was terrified of the water and knew that she was drowning when the canoes sped toward her. Rikki laughed at her and told her she was chicken. They watched the Royal Barge Spectacle on the river and walk -ed until Carmen's feet blistered and she was exhausted.

They visited the Samoan Exhibit and Carmen found her look-a-like there. The woman was over six feet tall but looked enough like Carmen to be her sister. The father insisted to tell Carmen and Rikki some of their history. Carmen was awed and inspired by their story.

They were treated to a Rick Shaw ride to the first aide station. Carmen's feet were treated and Rikki had some cool water. Once they were revived, the next stop was for pictures in grass skirts. Carmen shared one with a huge Hawaiian and they laughed their heads off. They ended their day with a delicious dinner feast in a lovely, natural setting. overlooking the sea.

The women boarded the bus in the evening

sated with food, excited by their day and with very sore
feet. She took a shower and afterwards offered to go
down to the bar with Hugh for a drink. He said he had
been on the beach and in the bar all day. Besides the
game would be on soon and he just wanted a beer while
he watched it in the room. Carmen took her tired self
and sore feet to bed.

The next morning Hugh did get up and had
breakfast with Carmen at a lovely Breakfast Bar around
the corner from the hotel. They strolled a little way
down Kealakekua Avenue and cut across Lewers Street
to the beach. They sat on the beach for awhile talking
and agreed to meet for dinner. Hugh went back to the
Sheraton and Carmen continued her stroll.

She decided to join the Waikiki Trolley Tour and
take in the sights along the route. She could always
come back later or get off at a stop and take the next trolley if she saw something that really caught her attention.
She spent the most enjoyable day alone. She had rarely
spent time alone and this was a novelty.

The Hawaiians responded to her ready smile and
open personality. They all volunteered tidbits of information about places and things they thought would interest her. As they passed a fabric shop, she asked the driver
to stop. An old Chinese lady also got off and offered to
go with her to make sure that she wasn't cheated. The
old woman even helped her choose several lengths of
lovely fabric. Carmen was charmed and thanked her pro-
fusely for her help.

She boarded the trolley once more and decided to
make the Hilton Hawaiian Village her last stop. She was

walking through the Shopping Arcade window shopping. As she passed the Ferragamo shop, a familiar fragrance wafted to her on the breeze. Longing washed over her in a tidal wave and she could 'see' Gus vividly before her.

I will not think of him. I cannot think of him. I came here to get him out of my system, how could I be so weak that a smell can conjure him up. I am not that needy. Hugh may not be what I want but he's what I have. I better be damn grateful and mindful of that every-day.

She wandered to the garden and found a seat. She sat there hugging herself and squeezing her legs clo-sed as the feelings she had been hiding from so long washed over her. She fantasized for a brief moment of how his big hands would feel holding her. She knew even though she was a big woman that she would fit in his arms perfectly and that his hands would know exactly how to hold her. And where he should touch her.

Why are we always needing and wanting what is not ours to have Lord? Why can't I need and want the man you gave me? Why has another invaded my mind, skin and body? Thank you for removing temptation out of my way, I could never, ever move myself.

She went back to the hotel and cajoled Hugh into making love to her. It's funny she thought as he worked to come. I now know that there is a difference between making love and having sex. I am forty-five years old and have never made love. I may not have the right, but I can't help wishing just once I could feel the difference too. Or at least feel something.

When Hugh rolled over and began to snore, she went into the bath and took a luxurious bubble bath. then dried off and went out to the terrace. She took her novel and coke to the lanai.

Carmen read her novel until she began to doze. She lay there, twenty stories above the earth, and watched the stars twinkle over Diamond Head until she fell asleep.

Chapter Five

Gus and Candace had an uneventful flight to San Francisco. Candy was quiet but she did talk a bit to Gus on the flight. She was starting to think about retirement and asked him for his advice on her pension plan. He was something of an expert on pension systems and she was smart enough to know that when he started to think about her problem, she didn't have to say another word.

She was concerned about spending ten days in close quarters with her husband. He knew her well and would nag her to distraction out of his concern. "I will have to tell him soon," she thought to herself. "I cannot keep this to myself much longer. Linda said Courtney would settle down by the time we get back home. I don't believe it. She is as stubborn as her Dad; she will never let it go." She closed her eyes and slept.

Her uneasy sleep was fraught with sighs. Gus gathered her close as the tears tracked across her cheeks. He stroked her hair back from her face as the plane winged it's way westward as Gus prayed for the answer to his wife's problem. He thought that he had always been there for her, but realized that somehow he had failed her. Maybe some time spent with her family would help. He sincerely hoped so. If not, the surprise trip he had planned for them to Honolulu should cheer her up.

As he settled down to sleep, Candy murmured so low that he almost missed the words.

"Oh Troy what should I do, I can't live like this anymore. I need to tell Gus about Courtney. I can't live a lie any more but I can't destroy his faith in us. I can't live with him hating us. I don't think I even want to live anymore Troy, I know I don't want to live."

The tears rolled silently down her cheeks as she slept. His heart broke for her. Thirty years of loving would not go away in an instant, so he held her and asked God for an answer. And when it came, the courage and strength to deal with it

On Tuesday Gus had asked Candace if she'd like to spend a few days in Honolulu with him. She had demurred and against his better judgment he had left her with her mother and father and flew to Hawaii alone He had come through on his way to Vietnam and back, but never had the opportunity to see the island. Something was pulling him to Pearl Harbor. Maybe he needed the hushed and hallowed setting of the Memorial to calm his restless spirit. Maybe he would find some of the answers he sought in that sacred place. His did know that being with Candace at this time wasn't really a solution.

There was still the problem of Courtney (his godchild and his niece)? He loved her and nothing her parents (he winced at the word) had done, could or would change the love in his heart for that precious little girl. How did he tell her the truth? She had come to him for an answer; did he have the right to give it to her?

What in the hell was he going to do? How was he supposed to feel about his *brother* Troy. Was he to believe it only happened once? And knowing them both , how they must have suffered. Holding this secret all of these years. I have to believe them. They are both good people. I am sure Troy has suffered as much as Candace. It must really hurt him to see his daughter and not be able to claim her.

I can easily understand how this happened. But why couldn't Candy come to me. Surely she didn't think I would blame her. I have no right to blame anyone the way I feel about Carmen. Thank God we will never have an opportunity tor temptation. I know I could never resist tasting those lips or molding those curves to my body.

Had he failed Candy and his family? They were all good people caught in an untenable situation. Probably waiting for him to see it himself. He never weld have seen it or thought it. Candace was a good woman and Troy was a good friend. He knew his wife. Whatever happened would not have been deliberate. She was not capable of deceit.

Troy was the only "brother" he had. He knew that an explanation would come and he had to be ready to accept it. Whatever it was. He could not allow one act of indiscretion to tear this family apart.

He hadn't even looked at another women in over thirty years. And right about all he could think about was Carmen.

"You're fifty-five years old man," he told himself over and over. "You ought to be able to figure this thing out without going mad. Maybe I need to talk to someone who can bring some objectivity to this mess."

He rented a car at the airport and checked into a

lovely motel set a few yards from the beach in Haleiwa.

After a swim in the ocean he explored the small town and had dinner. On the spur of the moment he decided to drive into Waikiki and look up an old Army buddy from Chicago.

His friend Noland worked at the Hilton Hawaiian Village in the shopping arcade. Gus strolled through the arcade window-shopping until he found his friend behind the counter in Farrago's. "Hey Buddy," Gus called. "What are you looking at? I came all the way over here to see you and you're looking at some woman."

"She is some woman all right, and taking the risk of sounding like a sixteen-year old, M sure wish she was mine, uh huh! What brings you all the way to Hawaii man? We haven't seen each other since Nam."

"I needed some peace and quiet. I also wanted to see Pearl Harbor and you in that order."

"What's wrong my brother? Care to drop the façade and talk to me? I get off in ten minutes. We can go to my place, have a few drinks and talk about the old days."

"Sounds like a plan, the only problem is, I'm driving. I don't know about here but the Man don't look kindly to mixing the two on the Mainland."

"Last I looked that didn't play here either. Why don't we go by my place and let me pick up a change of clothes. We'll get drunk and I'll drive in with you in the morning."

Gus agreed and he and his buddy Noland spent the night drinking and reminiscing. Gus had trusted Noland with his life in Nam. He decided to share his problem with him. Maybe the perspective would change viewed from another angle and through a haze of Napoleon Brandy.

He laid out the problem and identified the players. The two of them then looked at the situation from every possible angle, agreeing that hurt on all sides could not be avoided, but that Courtney's well being was top priority.

They also agreed that the situation with Candace was approaching the critical stage and that whatever Gus decided to do would have to be done ASAP and that Troy's help would have to be elicited. Gus told him that he loved Troy. The two of them had been friends from their teens and they had always had each others back.

He could not find himself being angry with him. But wasn't sure how to get this betrayal 'thing' out of the way. Those feelings had to be dealt with before any kind of healing could take place. And there was Carmen.

He told him who she was and the impact she had made on his life. He told his Buddy that if there was ever a woman made for him, it was she. He loved Candace, but he had fallen in love with Carmen on several levels. She was his soul mate but a relationship, other than business was impossible.

Nolan listened to him and told him that men would always be tested. Sometimes they passed with flying colors, other times they failed miserably. The main thing was to try and diminish the damage to all parties concerned. And above all; take care of the women and children. They finished the bottle and feel asleep where they were.

Early the next morning a seriously hung-over Gus headed for Pearl Harbor. He was almost late and had to run to catch the launch. He was the last one in line and helped the young navel ensign push it away from the pier. The launch was crowded but as he sat down he glimpsed a familiar hand, raised to the back of a woman's head. That gesture was the signature of the one person in the world that he never expected to see in this place, so he ignored it and put it down to the Brandy.

He settled back and absorbed the sight of the markers denoting the final resting place of the Pacific Fleet. They were dotted across the beautiful blue waters of Pearl Harbor. He listened attentively to the canned history lesson that issued from the speakers fore and aft.

He closed his eyes and felt that December Day settle in his sub-conscious. Gus knew somehow, that for more than one reason this day would live in his memory forever. He uttered a prayer of thanks for the opportunity to view this historic site. He vowed to bring his sons and grandsons here. They needed to feel the greatness of America and the bravery of it's people.

Carmen was deeply touched by her tour of the museum. She was especially moved by the plaque for Dorie Miller. She was from Brooklyn and had heard the story of the young black man who had gunned down a number of Japanese fighter planes at Pearl Harbor. The only jarring note to such a memorable occasion was an extremely rude and annoying young man.

He obviously had no idea of the significance of hallowed ground and seemed determined to ruin the day for the rest of the tour members. After being shushed by several of the ladies, two Shore Patrol's politely escorted him to the launching area and held him there.

The Arizona Memorial was one of the loveliest and most ethereal sights Carmen had ever seen. The white Memorial gently floated above the sunken hull starkly outlined in the crystal clear water. Fish swam in and out, and two Navy seals dove into the water at intervals. She couldn't help the eerie feeling that stirred the hairs on the back of her neck at the thought of the thousand or more men buried in the ship beneath her feet.

As she leaned against the rail, the tears started to fall unchecked. She smelled a familiar fragrance as the strong arms of her dreams enclosed her from the rear. She looked up to see Gus' eyes filled with tears, but his also held a soul wrenching pain. His arms tightened gently as she stirred and she quieted. Carmen reached up a hand and with her finger caught a tear as it fell from those beautiful lashes. She touched her finger to her mouth and kissed it, wiping the tears and the pain away in an instant.

Gus had never seen or felt anything so tender yet erotic in his entire life. He simply took her hand and led her over to the obelisk set into the lighted alcove that held the names of the military personnel who had given up their lives on that infamous day. They did not talk, simply held on to each other as they silently and speedily read as many names as they could quickly before giving their place to the next observer.

They boarded the launch in silence and sat together listening as one to the canned music issuing forth from the speakers. Gus helped his Lady from the launch and asked, "Would you come with me, I'd like to show you some special sights?"

"Oh yes! I really think we need some time to talk." Carmen spoke to the tour director and excused herself from the group. She and Gus walked back to the museum. They spent an hour absorbing the history of the place, memorizing each tiny detail of the day and absorbing each other into their pores. They left Pearl Harbor and traveled to the National Cemetery at Punch Bowl Crater. Once an active volcano, now the resting-place of some of our most famous national heroes.

"It is beautiful." Carmen whispered as they stood looking toward the steps leading to the Statue of Columbia. "I always want to cry when I think of the people buried here, but I've long realized that I am not crying for them but for me and my own immortality. Today I won't cry. I will remember this day, this place and you Gus, without sadness and pain."

"And I will remember you. Right now I am going to feed you and take you to the most beautiful spot on earth. There is a private garden in front, we can pluck and eat pineapple and kiwi from the trees. It is a special place where you stand in the living room and the ocean and sky is spread out as far as you can see. And you are only two or three steps from the beach. You can watch the sunset and see the water and sky blend into one. A place where you can gaze toward the horizon and cannot see the end. Am I making you hungry with this talk about fruit?

"I don't really want to eat Gus, I'd like to see this heavenly place instead, but if you're hungry?"He swung her around and molded her form to his. "Yes, my love I am hungry but not for food. I am trying to give you some space. You need to decide for yourself if you want to be with me today in this place.

I need you in a way that is beyond my compre-hension. I know that I will never, ever not need you or love you again, Carmen. Without claiming you, you are mine. Not as my girlfriend, not as my whore, not any-thing as banal as my woman. But as my "Special Lady. The woman who has laid claim to my heart and captured my soul. This is our one day out of a lifetime. One day to claim each other. I am hungry too, but definitely not for food

Gus stopped the car in a fragrant, secluded gar-den. Carmen could hear the ocean close by. The sound of the waves crashing on the shore matched the beating of her own heart. He stepped out of the car and reached out his hand. She felt the shock throughout her being. "Are you ready Baby?"

"Gus Honey, I've been ready since that evening on the terrace," she laughed. "I just couldn't admit it to myself. I don't want to eat, but, there are other things that can fill you up besides food!!!"

He swung her around and melded her soft curves, to his muscular frame. "Yes," she said with her heart shining in her eyes. "I was ready from the moment I saw you in that doorway. I knew that you were my present and my future. My being here with you now is as inevitable and necessary as each breath I've taken since that day."

"I love you, Carmen. I have fought myself and tried desperately to reason you away. I love my wife and I know that you love your husband. You are as obligated to Hugh as I am to Candace. I have prayed to be delivered of the fire that has burned inside me from the moment I first saw you. But I also prayed for one kiss, one thirst quenching drink from your sweet lips. He reached out his hand and touched her face. I have to have one touch of your satiny skin on mine. Maybe it will put that fire out forever."

"You realize that this may be the only day that we will ever have to consummate our love for each other? That we are in a business relationship and will see each other regularly, but will not be able to communicate our feelings by a word or touch."

He was raining kisses on her face and neck as he handed her out of the car. "Are you with me, Carmen? I know this is wrong but I can't help loving and wanting you. I feel that I will explode if I can not get into you right now."

"I feel you," she laughed, "and I believe you. But I still have enough sense left to know that there will be consequences. But I'm willing to deal with them tomorrow. Today belongs to us. We are a world away from our normal lives. After today , we will have to see each other, interact, know the power of this thing between us and ignore it. Can we do that? We will certainly have to find a way to deal with our feelings. But always remember that I love you."

Afterwards neither of them could recall how they ended up naked in bed. Carmen's head thrashed from side to side, as a tidal wave of feeling engulfed her. Her body convulsed each time he touched her, and a tidal wave of feeling engulfed her each time his lips or his hands made contact with her over-heated skin.

Each time he rubbed his leg along her thighs, she arched her back and offered him access to her soul. His kisses left a scorching trail of fire in their wake. He was afraid they would eventually be consumed. Gus reared like the wildest, untamed stallion being tamed by a wild and scented Valkyrie. He held her hands in his as he rode the winds of passion and fulfilled his wildest dreams.

"We are only going to have these few hours. They will belong to us for a lifetime. From here on we will be bonded in a way neither of us has ever experienced. But today is our once in a life " time out of time. He gathered her in his arms and told her: "You are my Lady now and forever in my care. I will be your friend and somewhere close by for the rest of my life.

If you ever need me don't hesitate to call and I will be right there." He pulled her sweat soaked body into his arms and tucked her head next to his heart. They spent ten precious minutes lying together, waiting for their hearts to beat normally again.
" Tomorrow we go back to our normal lives but the memory of what we've had here will be with us forever. I will keep an eye on you and if you ever need anything, I will see that you have it. If you are sick, I will know, because I too will be ill. You are mine, now and

forevermore."

They showered together and dressed. As they left their garden the sounds of Solomon Burke's, "Just Out of Reach" wafted across the water from a boat moored close to shore. The words written across their hearts.

The Ashley's last few days in Waikiki were uneventful. Carmen spent them on the Lanai of their room, writing some poems and working on her novel on her laptop. Hugh spent his time in the hotel bar watching the Yankees and any other sports event that happened to come on the big screen TV.

She was relieved to see the lights of the John F. Kennedy airport runway approach. She hadn't bothered to try and work on her novel during the long trip home. Hugh, between naps gave her a play-by play of each of his trips to the bar. He felt she had to know who won the game and how many sexy young girls had served him a drink. She'd listened to him with half an ear.

Her song was running through her head and she couldn't get rid of it. She finally gave in and accepted it and Gus as a part of her being and decided; "whatever will be, will be." She scribbled the words that seemed to be burned into her brain and across her heart into her diary.

You Are My Lady (He said to me...)

You are my lady... he said to me....
And I am your man, I am your man... for
eter...nity.
He came into my life, and he made me regret.
Vows to his brother, and older man, that I can't
forget.
The power of the ocean is in every kiss,
His touch is so real that it makes me feel,
e...ternal bliss.
You are my lady, and I am your man.
My love for you.... will make me do, all that I
can.
I'll change your whole life.... from pain, stress
and strife.
Make your dreams come true; and take care of
you,
though you're not my wife.
But you are my lady, he said to me.
And I am your man; I'll be your man for eternity.

I am your man, I'll be your man for eternity...

Carmen knew when she met him that Gus would change her life, just how had remained to be seen. Maybe, just maybe a platonic relationship could develop between them. They were grown, they should be able to work out a relationship. One without the physical and spiritual connection forged between them that day.

How ironic that after all of these years of wanting and needing a man that was her soul and bedmate, she had found the perfect one. Problem; they were both committed to others and there could be no thought of dissolving those relationships. Happiness could not be founded on the ruins of broken marriages and promises.

They were both basically good people. They had given in to their most primal urges and needs one time. That one time would have to last through eternity. Although she was sure God heard and saw His children's fall from grace, she still had to connect with Him. Ask his forgiveness and most of all ask him to shield her from further temptation.

It was time for one of her frequent chats with Him. She not only needed to ask His forgiveness for her lapse of fidelity. But she really needed him to provide some sort of guidance as to how she could live with such a huge emotional hole in her psyche.

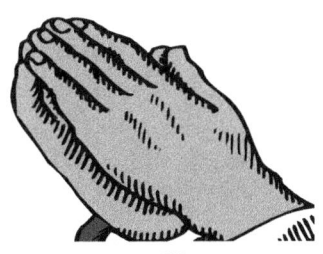

Chapter Six

On Monday morning Gus and Candace left San Francisco. They had spent some time alone on Sunday but the majority of the past four days had been spent with her family.

She appeared to have enjoyed her family, but the customary lift to her spirits had not really materialized. She still was unnaturally subdued. Ordinarily Candy would have reported all of the family news complete with comments and any new anecdotes involving her Dad, his grandchildren and his pets.

Today she opened a novel and began to read. This was a clear indication that she did not want to talk. He too opened T.D. Jakes latest book and read until he dozed off.

The flight to New York was smooth and good tail winds brought them home slightly ahead of schedule. Gus decided to take advantage of their early return and contact "his brother" Troy. He was curious to see how far he was willing to go to deal with this situation. He really wanted to see how much *information* he had gathered about the child's parents This whole problem was complicated, but they were all grown-ups. It was time to stop playing games and evading the truth.

He knew that this was his call. It was time he brought it out into the open. Candace was becoming more unstable by the day. He was seriously concerned about her health. prepared to step up to the plate.

He dropped his bags in the vestibule and used the living room phone to make his call. "Hey Man, we just got home. Did anything happen while I was gone that I need to know right now."

Troy was surprised to hear Gus's voice. He wasn't sure just when they were expected to return and didn't feel ready to tell his "friend" any new lies.

"Uh Hi Bro. I didn't expect you back yet. What happened, they ran out of rum punch or Wahinis? I'm on my way to a meeting right now. By the way, why are you all back so soon? Is Candace all right?"

Gus listened patiently as Troy rattled on. He realized that Troy must be nervous or uncomfortable with Him and wondered had he always been that way or was he seeing his "Brother" through different eyes. "I need to talk to you Man. What say we meet later tonight? But I need to help Candace unpack and get settled first."

"Okay Man, you sure you don't want to wait until tomorrow for this?"

Gus was emphatic in his answer. "Troy I don't want to wait until tomorrow or the next day. I need to talk to you now. Meet me at Brooklyn Slim's in fifteen minutes."

Gus did not really want to confront his Compadre. He knew that he had to do it and get it over with. He left the house and in ten minutes was slipping into a parking place across from the bar on Rogers Avenue. He crossed the street and entered the popular watering hole. He had deliberately chosen a place where neither of them was well known and wouldn't be disturbed by acquaintances dropping by the table as they talked.

"Hey Man how was your trip?" Troy greeted his "Brother." Gus held up his glass and the waiter brought him another brandy.

"Sit down Troy, you already asked me how was the trip. This is serious. Did you speak to Linda yet?

"Hold up Gus. give me minute here. I did speak to Linda and we decided that Courtney is not ready for this yet, even though she may think that she is. You know that the things children think they want are not always the things that they really need?" Linda is a good mother and only wants what is best for Courtney. Try and make your niece understand that, Gus. Did Candace tell you who the parents were?"

"No Troy, I figured it out on my own. Just let me talk, okay! This is the most difficult conversation I will ever have with you, my Brother. What I say may destroy our friendship of forty years and is certain to change it. I don't know if you ever thought in those terms, I suspect that you did at some point. Let me take a stab at guessing the names of Courtney's parents. I know that the *mother* is *my wife* Candace, and I am dead certain that you, *my brother, my friend* and *my attorney* are the father. Correct me here if I am wrong."

Troy stared at his friend with an expression that would have been comical in other circumstances. Guilt, chagrin, pain and loss flickered across his face. He attempted to speak several times, but lifted his hands in surrender. After clearing his throat Troy finally spoke.

"To say I am sorry for what happened is totally inadequate. The most difficult thing in my life has been having to face you nearly every day for the past fifteen years, knowing what I had done to you. First of all, please don't blame Candace for any of this mess. It is too late to ask you to forgive me. Let me try and explain how this happened."

Gus knew that he had to be fair and tolerant. He had to give Troy a chance to explain what had happened. He was really in no position to judge anyone. Troy's story had to be told in order for them to sort out this mess."

"Your Desert Storm assignment was extremely difficult for Candace. She depends on you for everything and missed you terribly. In addition to that your son Jon reacted to your absence by rebelling. He thought that he was the man of the house and refused to listen to his mother."

Sixteen year old boys need a firm man's hands close by all of the time. When he got really disrespectful to her, Candace called me. I managed to pull him out of a serious scrape. Then had to have several talks with Jon before I finally got him straightened out. Candace called me because next to you, I am the only other man who has been constantly present in the boy's life."

"You had told me to keep an eye on them . At first that is all it was. Later on her Mom got sick. She died shortly after and I helped her and Linda deal with the funeral and disposal of her house. I got in the habit of dropping around to change light bulbs and do minor repairs. Mavis never needed me to do any of those kind of things. She and her brothers took care of my house. I felt pretty good being able to help Candace out."

One evening she was upset. We were sitting in your living room talking and she started to cry. I held her and one kiss led to another. We ended up making love. She was ashamed and I was disgusted with myself. I should have known better. We were both pretty upset."

"Don't think that I'm trying to say that you set this up. We did not have an affair. One night we found ourselves in a situation that got out of hand. "Neither of us even thought of a lasting relationship and could not handle the guilt of an extended relationship. I don't expect you to believe me and I certainly don't deserve anything from you except a punch in the face."

We both cared too much about you to get involved in an affair. When Candace found out she was pregnant, she became depressed and actually talked about suicide. She knew that she couldn't keep the baby. I really wanted the child, but Mavis walked out the moment I told her about the baby. "

"I did not want to, but I suggested an abortion or adoption. You know your wife well enough to understand why she chose to have the baby. I offered to take the child and give it to one of my Auntie's in Jamaica to raise.

I had resigned myself to being fatherless, but now this miracle had occurred. I had to find a way to have some claim to my child."

"Candace could not handle an abortion emotionally. We all knew that Linda always wanted a baby, but you and I have always known that she was a lesbian. We found the perfect solution and chose the best way out for all concerned. Linda and Candace look enough alike to be twins. You wouldn't be likely to question her having a child that that looked exactly like her. We didn't tell you Courtney was adopted because of her close resemblance to Linda and Candace."

"It was natural for me to be the other godfather because you were not here, I was. This way it was natural for me to love and help care for her. I have always wanted kids. I am the favorite uncle and godfather for all of the children in your family. This arrangement would allow me to be close to my daughter as she grew up. And I could always contribute to her support."

Candace and I both would always be close to the child. Nobody was likely to question the child's birth, even you. Candace would see her daughter every day and participate in her life. We did not count on was Candace's guilt-driven depression or Courtney's curiosity.

I certainly never expected to have a civilized conversation with you about it. I have gone over this moment in my mind every day for the past fifteen years and can only say that men sometimes do things that are clearly wrong, but regret them for the rest of their lives. I am truly sorry for betraying your trust.

Gus was at a loss for words. He was feeling so many things, sorrow, betrayal, empathy (he too had committed adultery) and helplessness. What could he do to sort out this mess? "Troy, hold it a moment. I am trying to absorb all of this. I literally owe you my life and cannot forget that. I counsel others in similar situations. Now that it's home, I can't seem to think this through. I have to find a way to come to terms with all of this."

"It makes no sense to throw away forty years of friendship, love and shared memories (not to mention a business and fraternal relationship) because of one mistake. For the moment, I agree that we all have to decide how Courtney is to be dealt with. She has a right to know about her parents, but I also agree with you that if this is not done right, the child can suffer severe emotional trauma."

"My first response will be to Candace. I am fearful for her now more than ever. This has to have taken a serious emotional toll on her limited resources. We really need to work fast. Give me a few days to research our situation.

I need you to produce the legal documents regarding the birth I also want your position re: Child support and heir status. You have no other children, but Mavis is going to try to destroy you financially. I don't want the child caught between you two. I want to get all of the adults (including her *Brothers)* together by the weekend.

Troy tentatively held out his hand, but pulled it back before Gus could reject him. "It's your call Bro. I'll go along with whatever you want to do. We were all concerned about your reaction because you are so honorable and we had betrayed you. Not just by the affair, but also by covering up the facts of Courtney's birth. I don't know what to say except that I don't want to lose you as a 'Brother' or the best friend that I have ever had. I will ask you to forgive us both. We have all suffered and Candace is now near the breaking point. Courtney is my only biological child. I have had to deny her and stand on the periphery of her life while she grew up fatherless.

The child has made you her father/substitute. I appreciate the job that you have done. Who better to be her surrogate father than you. Once she knows the truth, our positions may shift in her head. She will have to sort everyone out and re-assign our places in her mind. I, frankly am afraid of how she places us."

Gus clapped him on the shoulder then handed him the check. "Your mess Man, these drinks are on you," he said as he walked out the door. He drove the few blocks home slowly, mentally gearing himself up to face his wife. He also needed to do some research to prepare himself for the upcoming meeting. It would be up to him to find a workable solution to this god-awful situation.

Carmen bounced into her office on Monday morning, rested and ready to get back to work. She had spent Sunday evening with Vanessa and Shawn giving them a blow-by-blow description of their trip. She had them hysterical from her story of the bikini bottom and the big wave and the picture of her in a grass skirt with a big, fine Hawaiian man.

She described Diamond Head in detail and her trying to squeeze through a volcanic fissure. They all cried at her description of the solemn beauty of Punch Bowl Crater military cemetery with the majestic stairs leading to the statue of Columbia. She told them as majestic as they were, she didn't climb them because her feet wouldn't let her.

She described the Luau and Yacht Party in detail, and her trip to the Polynesian Village. The trip to the Village resulted in the largest toe blister the guide had ever seen, and ended in a wild ride to the first aide station with a fine Australian medic. They laughed through her shopping trips through the various malls and the Flea Market at the Aloha Bowl.

She omitted the Hilton Mall and Pearl Harbor and that life-changing day with Gus. Shawn had carefully watched her mother through the laughter and the stories. She realized that something else had happened, but knew that her mother would not tell her until she was good and ready. She wondered if her Dad had finally gotten on her Mom's last nerve a thousand miles away from home. Whatever it was, she was certain that Vanessa did not need to know.

She had finally told Luis a definite yes, so the wedding was on. Her mom and sister were thrilled.

The remainder of the evening was spent making hasty but tasteful plans for her shotgun wedding.

Erica was already at her desk sorting mail when Carmen arrived at the office. "Welcome home Boss Lady. We really missed you around here. Roseatta and I took good care of your plants. Now what did you bring us?"

"We will wait until break time when Roseatta can be with us. Suffice it to say that we had a lovely time. Now let's get down to business. Schedule an appointment for me with Mr. Ames and set up my monthly meeting with our vendors. How is the communications project going?"

"Everything went well. Adam is almost as good at trouble-shooting as his boss and we worked on it together. They will be finishing up soon. Do you need an exit appointment with Mr. Hayden and Adam?"

"That is a good idea, since you and Adam are working on it too, schedule the meeting for the four of us and Jake Ames. Use the small conference room and call the caterers and have a lunch or dinner with drinks prepared."

The women worked steadily for the next few hours, going over schedules, setting up appointments and prioritizing phone calls. Carmen took a break to call home and check on Hugh. "Hi Honey, did you finish unpacking?"

"Carmen, you gave me fifty things to do. I can't do everything. Luis is here to take me to the ballgame.

I'll unpack later."

"Where's Shawn. I need to speak with her?"

"She's in the bathroom throwing up again. You need to tend to that. It's gone on too long. I tried to give her some Chamomile tea but she wouldn't take it. She better not let anything happen to that baby. Luis is here, bye.

"Good Lord, isn't it just like that man to hang up before I'm done," Carmen fumed. "I don't know why I married that old man in the first place. He's going to drive me nuts." She hit the redial button and Shawn answered. "Hi Baby, do you feel any better?"

"Yes Ma, I think it's more wedding jitters than baby now. Thanks for hooking up the Temple so fast. Uncle Jake must be a real big shot over there. Tell him I said thanks."

"I will Sweetie. I have to run but I wanted to check on you before I got too busy."

"Okay Pretty Lady. I will call if there are any new developments."

Carmen asked Erica to order lunch for Roseatta and herself. They could rehash her trip while eating.

Roseatta breezed into the room dressed in an outfit more suited to Carnival than the office." Hi Ms. C. good to have you home. Like my outfit? I wore it in your honor, don't I look Hawaiian?" She didn't give Carmen a chance to answer. "Did you know Mr. Hayden was there too? I saw him a few minutes ago and he said that he was in San Francisco with his wife. Then he went to visit his friend in Honolulu and they toured Pearl Harbor. Did you go to Pearl Harbor too, Ms. C?"

"Yes I did, I toured Honolulu from Diamond Head to Pearl Harbor.

"Settle down, and I'll tell you all about my trip." The ladies laid out their Chinese feast and listened raptly to hilarious stories of Carmen's Hawaiian Adventure. They especially liked the one about her Samoan look-a-like and sharing a grass skirt with the big Hawaiian dancer.

They laughed hysterically when she told them how scared she got in the Imax Theater when she thought the canoes were coming right at her.

Later in the afternoon Carmen ran into Adam, the young man from Hayden Enterprises in the hallway outside her office.

"Good afternoon Mrs. Ashley, good to see you again. Did you enjoy your vacation?"

"I did indeed Adam. How did our project go in my absence?"

"Everything is right on track. Erica and I worked well together. She took care of organizing your staff and I saw to it that they were trained. That Erica is really something else, Mrs. C."

"Why thank you Adam. I will be sure and tell her

you said so. By the way, how is your boss?

"To tell you the truth I really don't know. Something seems to be wrong, but Mr. Hayden ain't likely to tell me his personal problems. See you later Mrs. Ashley. Erica and I have some work to do."

Carmen went back to her office and completed her afternoon appointments. She didn't get another chance to think about Gus or the problems she knew he was trying to work out. She had a Community Board meeting that night, so she did not bother to go home. She was afraid that she would get caught between Hugh, Shawn and wedding drama. She would much rather deal with tangible and fixable issues.

The State was bringing a homeless shelter into their neighborhood. Her neighborhood was already inundated with social service facilities. Carmen was one of the chief planners of a March and Demonstration on the Mayor's office. She spent a couple of productive hours working out the logistics with some of the committee members. They decided to use a two pronged approach and take it to the developer's office at the same time. They finished their work around nine and she left for home. It had been a long day.

Bessie did her a favor and started after only a few coughs and sputters. She thought briefly that Jake and Gus were right. She was going to have to buy a new car soon. However, she had a wedding and baby in the very-near future. Her finances did not include a car.

Hugh was glued to the TV set in the living room and barely acknowledged her. "Hi Hugh, I'm home."

She dropped her bags in her office and went to look for Shawn. Her daughter was in her room surrounded by wedding paraphernalia. "Hi Baby, what did you manage to get done today?"

"Hi Ma, I am so excited. Look at all of this stuff. "V" and I went to Pearl's and Michaels and found everything that we need for the decoration and favors. Are you going to do the flowers and the capia's for my guests?"

"Of course; I was just waiting for you to ask." She spent the rest of the evening helping design the various decorations and floral pieces for the wedding. By midnight they were both drooping and ready for bed. She hugged her daughter and went to her own room to prepare for bed.

She stepped into the shower and as the water cascaded over her body, Gus popped unbidden into her mind. "Go away Mr. H. I have too much on my plate to deal with you right now. Never the less, just thinking about him caused a heaviness to settle in the juncture of her thighs. Her nipples started to tingle and she closed her eyes. As the water sluiced over her body, she felt his hands trace the waters path. Her mind (as always) warred with her emotions.

Common sense and a sense of loyalty to Hugh made her feel guilty (the man was right in the next room for God's sake). Never the less she relished the feel of Gus's hands on her body. Even more or at least as much as making love to Gus, she loved talking to him. He was intelligent, a great conversationalist and a good listener. He was also funny in a dry and obscure way. Gus could tell a joke with a completely dead face. She would crack up and he would look at her and ask, "what's so funny?" His expression would not have changed.

They had talked about everything under the sun. They shared confidences and told each other their secrets. She knew that he had to care a great deal for her to open up and share as much of himself as he did in those three precious hours.

She acknowledged there in the privacy of her shower stall, that she was in love with him. Of course there would never be anything else between them but friendship. There would not even be occasional stolen moments like those they had shared in paradise.

They were married to other people and the price of their love would come too high. But somewhere deep inside behind the layers of common sense, morality and duty lay a wild inextinguishable flame of hope.

Hope that someday, some way she could be with Gus (whom she knew now...way too late) was the man of her dreams, forever.

She stepped out of the shower and found her husband stark naked, spread-eagled on the bed. He was waiting for her. "what the hell,? she thought. The man is my husband and I guess he has to get some, sometime. I'm lucky to have a man of my own that I can turn to when my fantasies don't materialize. I may as well get this over with. "Are you waiting for me?" She asked her husband. "This just might be your lucky night."
"I knew you'd come if I waited long enough Carmen. Now what do you want to do?"

Gus had taken a few days off work after his return from the West Coast to research their situation. He had spent the past few weeks reading everything that he could find on the psychological effects of adoption on children.

Since most States allowed adoption records to be open, many adopted children were now looking for their birth parents. Sometimes the reunions turned out all right, with others the parties on both sides ended up hurt and disillusioned.

Their situation was particularly hairy as the people involved were all so close. Candace was already being acknowledged as Courtney's aunt and godmother and Troy her godfather. His sons were her cousins and she was the beloved baby of both families'. Gus was the acknowledged patriarch of both families'. He loved them all and had always been the designated protector/problem solver for their family and friends.

He wanted desperately to talk to Carmen about this situation. He had found that she had an uncanny ability to bring clarity to difficult situations. He also knew that seeing her would only make him want her more. He had not been successful in wiping her out of his mind or heart, but he never wanted to hurt her or be unfair to her.

Seeing his "Lady" would be painfully difficult for them both. He definitely did not want to cause her hurt in any way, but sometimes he couldn't help wonder what she was doing . Thank God Adam (his assistant), talked so much. He often picked up bits of information about Carmen via him through his friend Erica. He wondered if Carmen thought of him as often as he thought of her and if they could put their sexual fantasies aside long enough to maintain a platonic relationship. He fervently hoped so because he never wanted her out of his life again.

"Hi Mr. Hayden, this is Erica, Mrs. Ashley would like to set up an exit interview with you and Adam to discuss the communications project outcome. Is next Friday at one o'clock okay with you?"

"One o'clock is fine young lady. Is there any particular area Mrs. Ashley needs clarification on?"

"I don't think so. Mr. Ames will be here also. It's more of a debriefing and opportunity to discuss other areas that need improvement."

"I will be there with Adam at one on Friday."

"Thank you Mr. Hayden."

"Adam", Gus called through the doorway. "We have an appointment with Mr. Ames and Mrs. Ashley on Friday at one. Call the florist and have a palm tree delivered to Mrs. Ashley and flowers to Erica. Also send my friend Jake a box of good cigars.

Have it all delivered on Friday morning with the compliments of Hayden Enterprises. Get me your notes so that we can have an overview of the project prepared. I have some suggestions of other ways that we can maximize their existing systems. I want your ideas too.

"I'm right on it Mr. Hayden."

Gus settled back in his chair and thought of all of the things that he wanted to say to Carmen when he saw her. He had gotten all of the adults concerned together to talk about the situation. He included his sons Gus and Jon because their family dynamics had changed also.

They met at Linda's house around her dining table. Gus explained why they were there and assured Candace that he and Troy had talked about the situation and they planned to maintain their relationship just as it was. The two families were tied together tightly and one tragic incident would not break those bonds.

He assured Candace that he did not hold either of them responsible for what had occurred but they all needed to focus on Courtney and her need to know the truth about her birth.

Candace had finally calmed down a little. She was ready to accept the fact that her secret was now out in the open and that she was not alone. She had others to help her tell Courtney the truth and deal with her reaction.

Troy assured them all that he was ready and willing to accept her as his child. He was financially sound and she was his heir. He also informed them that he had been helping Linda all along under the guise of Godfather.

The main problem as they all saw it was whether Courtney would be able to reassign the roles of her mother and aunt, accept Troy as her father and her cousins to her brothers. They agreed that Gus would make the initial explanation with Candace and Linda present.

He had tried to get up the courage to call Carmen and ask her how would she handle Courtney? Maybe there would be a chance for them to talk after the meeting. He felt good just knowing that he would see his Lady soon. I am in love with her and I need her. I may as well accept the fact and understand that business is all we have.

On Friday morning Carmen dressed carefully. She was nervous as a cat and excited as a teenager on her first date. She had trouble applying her make-up and changed her dress three times. She finally settled on an electric blue knit with long sleeves and a softly draped cowl collar. The sleeves and collar was slashed with black suede and she slipped into matching black and blue suede sling backs. She added dangling silver earrings studded with sapphires. Then pulled her hair up in a ponytail and secured it with a royal blue and silver banana clip.

"Hold it Pretty Lady," Shawn called to her as she gathered her purse and tote bag. "Where are you going all gussied up?"

"I have an important meeting this afternoon, if you really need to know ."

"Who's it with, Denzel Washington?"

"No it is not. I am meeting with Mr. Ames and Mr. Hayden, one of our vendors."

"The same man that was in Hawaii Ma?"

"How did you know?" Carmen asked her impatiently. "Shawn, I don't have time for this. I have to get to work."

"Take it easy Mama, I was just teasing you. By the way, you look great. Have a good day, Okay."

"You too Baby. Hugh, I'm gone." She called toward the kitchen.

"Bye Carmen, I'm going to the game this afternoon with Luis."

"Have a good time. I'll see you later."

She ran to her car and Bessie started on queue. "I got out of there just in time. I am not up to answering Miss Shawn's questions about my business this morning. Thanks Bessie old girl. Mama's treating you to an overhaul real soon." Her parking space was vacant for a change, she parked quickly and whisked into her office. She was in good spirits. "Good morning Erica, is everything set for our meeting this afternoon?

"Morning to you too, Boss Lady. Don't you look the sexy executive today? You smell good too!"

"Did I miss your birthday? Who sent you the flowers/"

"They came from Hayden Enterprises, they sent you and Mr. Ames something too! Go on check out your office."

Carmen was greeted at her door by a six-foot tall Palm tree festooned with white orchids. The delicate smell took her right back to the garden in Haleiwa. "Oh Gus, thank you," she whispered into the fragrant palm.

She called to Erica to bring her first cup of coffee and started her day. Occasionally as she worked, her eyes would stray to the palm tree that now dominated her office garden.

At twelve-thirty Erica went into the small conference room to set up for the meeting. Adam came early to help her and get in the way. Carmen decided to make a quick call home to check on Shawn and Hugh.

"Hi Hugh, how are you two doing today? Is Luis there yet?"

"Shawn's in her room and Luis isn't here yet. What do you want?"

"I was just checking to see if you were alright. Tell Shawn I called, I will call her again later."

"Okay Carmen, I gotta go now."

She hung up her phone, and looked up to see Gus standing in the doorway. Her heart lodged in her throat as she drank in the sight of him. "Hi Gus, I didn't know you were there. How are you and your family?"

"I'm fine Carmen. How's Shawn coming along? Ready for that wedding yet?"

"Why are we standing here making small talk when all I want to do is fall into his arms and let him kiss me senseless", Carmen thought.

"Why am I standing here talking when I should have her in my arms, instead of standing here like the true idiot that I am," Gus thought.

They took a step toward each other just as Erica called out; "Mrs. Ashley, we're almost ready. Do you need some help with your things?"

"I,I,I'm alright (she stuttered), Mr. Hayden will help me."

"I need to talk to you about Courtney after the meeting. Do you think that you can spare me an hour this afternoon?   I met with Troy the night I came home and the other adults last week. Candy seems a bit better, but something tells me she is on an emotional ledge. She can't stay there much longer."

"I'll be glad to, I hope that I can be of some assistance."

"Just talking to you may bring some clarity and objectivity to the situation. I am much too close to all of the participants in this drama and God knows that child is like one of my own. I have two boys and she is the daughter that I have always wanted.

I also want to offer you my assistance for your daughters wedding. It seems to have turned into a much larger undertaking than you originally planned. Is there anything else you may need help with?"

"I think we have it under control, at least for now. It's time to get inside Carmen wondered what he meant by 'anything else', Erica called her again.

Seeing his *"Lady"* on the job would be painfully

difficult for them both, but they would have to play it off. They could not take the chance of anyone finding out about their stolen hours in Hawaii. From the looks of it Adam and Erica really worked well together and wasn't *seeing* anything but each other.

"Coming right now", she answered.

The meeting was a success. The young people had obviously done their jobs well. Jake Ames was pleased to see his two favorite people working so well together. He came up with a number of new ideas that he wanted them to explore.

The suggestions that Gus and Adam made were well-received and Erica and Adam had also come up with some interesting ideas. Gus was alert to Carmen's every movement and hung to her every word. "I'm so glad just being in the same room with her. I am more than happy simply being her friend. And whether she knows it or not, her protector too."

Gus prayed silently to himself, "Lord I have ask-ed you for forgiveness for my lapse in fidelity. I want to thank you for the gift of Jake's friendship and through him, Carmen. She needs a friend and so do I. We will be good for each other. And on my honor, there will be nothing more. My greatest concern is for your daughter Candace. I ask that you guide me through this. Help me say and do the right thing for the ones you've placed in my protection; all of them….Amen.

She had been aware of his every movement and word throughout the afternoon, and looked forward to spending a few moments alone with him. She had already talked herself into an understanding of the parameters of he relationship and decided that if the only way she could have him in her life was as a business colleague and personal friend, so be it.

She couldn't really manage an affair and face God, Hugh and herself (in that order) each day. Carmen made a mental note to ask Gus if anything was brewing between Adam and Erica.

The meal was filled with lively conversation. Erica insisted that Carmen rehash her exploits in Hawaii and Jake wanted to hear how Gus had reacted to Pearl Harbor (he too had been in the military and was debriefed at Ft. DeRussey).

Gus described the Museum and Memorial in vivid detail. Erica was overcome with emotion when he described the wall with the names of the soldiers and sailors lost that day.

Carmen forgot that she hadn't told anyone that she had been there and spoke eloquently of the eerie feeling that she experienced standing and looking down into the water. She too had absorbed the feeling of loss and pain as the Memorial gently rocked gently back and forth over the hulk of the sunken ship Arizona. She was so engrossed with her description that she did not notice Jake, Erica and Adam exchanged a quizzical glance, then sneaked a look at the two of them. "Did you two run into each other that day, Jake inquired?" unaware of the undercurrents in the room.

"Yes we did," Gus answered quickly. "I had always wanted to see Pearl Harbor. The sight surpassed my expectations; I will tell you this, it is the one National monument that every American, regardless of race, origin or color should see. Black people would be so proud of Dorie Miller, by the way: did you know he was from Brooklyn?"

He talked fast to cover Carmen's obvious confusion at the unexpected questions. She recovered and joined in, making them laugh at the "big wave tale" and Hugh's beach bunny story.

Jake finally realized that the afternoon was gone and it was time to close the office. "I guess it's too late to get any more work done. "Gus, thank you for the new insight. Adam, it is a pleasure working with you. Erica you were great throughout this project and Rosetta, I couldn't function without you." The younger people all beamed at his praise. Erica asked to speak. Mr. Ames said of course.

"I just want to thank Mr. Hayden and Adam for the lovely flowers and Mr. Ames for our promotions and thank you Roseatta for teaching me how to take care of My Boss Lady."

Carmen spoke quickly before Jake herded everyone out of the room. "Mr. Hayden did you need to speak to me? He nodded in the affirmative. "Then let's return to my office, I need to be close to the phone."

He looked forward to spending a few moments after the meeting with her discussing his family situation.
Jake asked Gus to come into his office after he spoke to Carmen. He wanted him to check out some of

the new features on his Blackberry. "I'll be right there, Jake. Mrs. Ashley, that was one productive meeting, are you always so organized?"

"I try to be. I find comfort in order and I need order to be able to think. I also have Erica. You are no joke either, Sir."

"Carmen, I dumped a real problem on you in Hawaii and you haven't heard from me since. I met with Troy the night I came home and the other adults last week. Candy seems a bit better, but something tells me that the stress of the past fifteen years of worry has taken a toll on her.

She appears to me to be seriously shaky mentally. I don't know if exposing the situation made it any better. I suspect that it just may harm her further. What do you think? Should I take this off her altogether? I have always taken care of her problems. But she is the principal in this thing. She is Courtney's birth mother.

Courtney knows it now and neither of them seem to want to change anything. She's not capable of taking charge. Courtney is angry and I don't think she knows how to re-assign roles for us. Now she's dumping all of her anger on me and ignoring Troy altogether. I know that time will take care of this situation, but I wonder if we have any left.

Candace refuses to believe that I am not angry with her . No matter how many times I tell her that she is forgiven, she says that she can't forgive herself. I am really worried about her. Courtney will be sixteen in two weeks. She is driving me nuts. She wants me to tell her how she should feel about the situation, and sort out her Mama's and Daddy's. She is driving me crazy with her questions.

I am encouraging her to talk to the Lord and her Mama Linda. She will get guidance from one or both of them if she would only calm down. I am nearly at my wits end. Even Troy thinks I should give *him* some guidance.

Time is the enemy here. Candace is getting shakier mentally each day. I've tried my best to reassure her that this will all work itself out. I've prayed hard for some answers and I'm trying to get the others to do the same. I know today is not a good time to talk. But Carmen, I feel there is a time bomb ticking and only I hold the shut-off code."

Gus, I don't have anything else to offer you except my prayers. Courtney thinks she's grown. She is still a child who has opened the jar and spilled the contents. She wants them back in the jar, but once the contents are out; it's impossible to get them all back in that jar. You have done your job. Now you must let go and let God! He's a whole lot better at hinky problem-solving than you are.

"Lady you are really something. In five minutes you have raised questions that I have not quite formulated. I agree that Candace should talk to the child."

"I really have to run now. I have a Community meeting to that I must go to on my way home.

"Thank you Carmen. You did exactly what I thought you would. A conversation with you has pointed me in the right direction." He shrugged his shoulders, gave her a mock salute and left to speak with his friend.

She gathered her things and waved to Erica and Adam on her way out. They were engrossed in conversation and hardly noticed her departure.

Not so: As her boss walked away Erica whispered to Adam; "Is something going on that we don't know about?"

He replied; "If it is, we don't need to know it. Mr. Hayden is one of the most decent men that I know and Mrs. Ashley seems like a real lady. Just leave it here with us and don't mention anything you see to your nosy friend Roseatta."

Carmen stuck her head in Jake's door on the way out of the office. " Mr. Hayden, I am curious about something you said earlier. You said that I should let you know if I needed any other help with the wedding. I don't know what I may need at this point. I'm grateful for your offer, but Jake will be there for me."

" You didn't ask my Dear, Jake did. He needed the Temple quickly. I am the Master, so I cancelled a scheduled meeting. I didn't know at the time that it was for you. When he told me it was for your daughter I didn't mind making the arrangements to open and close for you. I'm just sorry I couldn't get the fee waived."

"Waiving the fee is unnecessary. Luis' family is fairly wealthy and is taking care of the largest expenses. Jake will be there as part of the family. You and your Brothers are invited to the Reception. You probably know some of my family members and friends anyway, Jake certainly does."

"My daughter Shawn and I both thank you. Since you will be there anyway, you and the Brothers present are invited and by all means bring young Adam with you."

"I'll accept your offer and remember if you need anything else, just tell Jake or call me. We will be there to open the place, set up and close for you. You will also get a chance to meet Troy and my sons."

"You are more than welcome. I'll see you in two weeks at the wedding, if not before. I hope things work out all right for all of you. You are a good man Augustus Hayden. Your family is lucky to have you. "

"She thought to herself; "He will find a way to resolve his problems. He must be accustomed to folks leaning on him. I'm about ready to do some leaning myself."

"Jake, tell Roseatta to call me in the morning. I'm going to take her up on her offer to cook some Jamaican dishes for the reception. Do you know if she bakes Black Cakes? Don't you forget the Champagne you promised,"

She closed her car door and drove off. She never noticed him behind her all the way to her meeting.

Chapter Seven

Carmen was extremely busy for the next two weeks. The race was on to get Shawn and Luis to the altar before the baby made her appearance on the scene. Shawn was eight months pregnant and her Daddy was too ashamed to have to walk down the aisle with her looking like Baby Hughey. They all tried to tell him that he didn't have to walk with her, one of her uncles would do it. But he didn't want that. Carmen concluded that he was jittery and scared that something was going to happen to stop the wedding.

Luis was underfoot any time he wasn't at work and Shawn vacillated from elation to downright evilness. The baby added her two cents worth by kicking her mother in extremely personal places at odd times. Vanessa was happy that her sister was saving her from the embarrassment of unwed motherhood. But, at the same time was jealous of all the attention that Shawn was getting.

Carmen's layette had to be put on hold because the wedding decorations was now priority. She wanted her baby to come home from the hospital in an outfit made by her Grandma. She took it to work and finished it on her lunch hour. That way all of her time at home could be dedicated to working on the wedding and calming frayed nerves.

She escaped the madness at home by going in to work early. On the Friday morning before the wedding Jake Ames came into her office. "Carmen, I hate to add to your problems right now, but have you seen or spoken to Gus Hayden recently?"

"No Jake, you saw him the last time I did, maybe I can help you?"

"I don't know. His wife called me this morning and I don't like the way she sounded. I know something is going on in the family. He told me that he had spoken to you and you had given him some advice. I wonder if that situation has come to a head and Gus need help in some way."

"I haven't heard from him but we will all be at the Temple tomorrow afternoon. He promised to open it for me. I doubt if there will be time for a real conversation but I will speak to him and tell him to call you. If I don't see him I will call you myself. Don't worry Jake, everything will be fine." Carmen spoke with a confidence that she did not feel.

Gus was dealing with a volatile situation that could explode in many directions. "Should I call him or not?"she dithered. "I will feel bad if I could do something to help and Just sat here. "Erica," she called into the intercom.

"Yes Ms. C, do you need me?"

"Please come here for a moment I need o ask you something."

Erica came into the office. "What's up Boss Lady?", she asked.

"Have you seen Adam or Mr. Hayden lately?"

"I saw Adam last night. I haven't seen Mr. Gus. Adam says he hasn't been in to work for most of the week."

"Do you know if he is ill?"

"Adam thinks something is wrong with Mrs. Hayden. He says that she has been acting real strange recently and that Mr. Gus is really worried."

"Thank you Erica." Carmen dug through her purse for the business card Gus had given her in Hale-iwa. It had his cell phone and private number. She dialed the cell phone first. Gus answered on the first ring.

"Hayden here," Gus answered brusquely.

"Thank God it's you. Gus it's m e Carmen, Honey what's wrong (the endearment slipped out unbidden). I'm worried about you."

"Hi Carmen, I'm sorry that you were worried. I planned to see you tomorrow and bring you up to date. I have my hands full right now. Can this talk wait until tomorrow? I'll tell you everything then."

"Jake is looking for you, you need to call him. He has something important to tell you."

"Thanks Carmen, I'll give him a call as soon as I can."

"Make time for him Gus, he may have something that will shed some light on your situation, okay?"

Carmen hung up the phone more perturbed than ever.

"Oh well, I will just have to wait until tomorrow to find out what's going on. I hope everything is going all right. I suspect that it isn't."

Gus really did have his hands full. After his talk with Carmen the previous week he had called Troy. The men had met over dinner and tried to work out the best way to help Candace. They agreed that nothing serious could be done abut her condition until she talked to Courtney, and the two of them worked out some kind of a relationship.

Linda was the only bright spot in all of this. She truly loved Courtney. She had already accepted the fact that high school graduation was coming up in two weeks. Courtney would be leaving home for college within the next two years. She also believed that they as a family unit, had grounded Courtney in love.

She would certainly miss her *daughter* but the love that had been showered on her for fifteen years would surface. The child would accept the situation and as she matured, would figure out how she felt about her *parents*. Linda, like Gus knew that she'd straighten out before too long.

Linda had already explained to the youngster the plus side of having not one, but three sets of doting parents. Those benefits to a youngster entering college should out-weigh any period of prolonged anguish. Besides they all knew that Courtney's naturally sunny personality would help her recover quickly.

As a "closet lesbian" Linda was well acquainted with feelings of hurt, frustration, disillusionment and pain . She was also a mental therapist. Her plan was to keep Courtney's room available and her heart open to her daughter. She also felt that the longer Candace delayed talking to the child, the greater the emotional fallout. When Troy told his wife. Mavis the whole story, she had immediately moved out of the house. She gone back to her family.

Troy had already been served with divorce papers. He had no intention of contesting the divorce. Their marriage had been over for years, They were just too comfortable to end it.

Gus had planned to preserve his marriage if Candace wanted to. The only problem left was to persuade Candace to talk to Courtney. Gus had arranged for all of the adults to meet at Linda's house tonight. When Carmen called, he was trying to reach Candace at work.

He planned to pick her up. Recently her driving had been erratic. She had nearly fallen asleep at the wheel on several occasions lately. He couldn't determine whether it was from the medication that she was taking for depression or the fact that she was mentally and physically exhausted.

Gus was glad that Carmen had called, just hearing her voice made him feel better. He was looking forward to seeing her tomorrow. In the past few months he had come to rely on her practical, common sense approach to problems and her quick wit. She was a wonderful woman, deeply committed to her family, friends and her community.

She was always looking for ways to help people. He suspected that it was often at her own expense. He thanked God for placing her in his life. And asked him everyday to forgive their indiscretion. He still could not find himself regretting it. He knew that made no sense.

That once in a lifetime day had forged a bond between them, one that would never be broken. They were now a part of each other (there would be no sexual part of the relationship) and would always be there for each other. Their business relationship and friendship would provide opportunities for them to spend some time together and share each other's lives.

He was glad to be able to help her out tomorrow and looked forward to meeting her friends and family. Later in the evening he crossed the driveway to Linda's house. The lights were blazing and Troy's Mercedes was parked in front. Candace was hanging back and Gus had to keep urging her forward. "Listen Baby, you are going to be alright. We are all here for you and Courtney. She is bound to be upset at first. We all love you both and are here to help you deal with her."

"What if she hates me Gus? I couldn't take that. I know I made a mistake, but she is a child. How do I know she'll understand?. How do I know she'll forgive me for giving her away?"

"You have to have faith Baby. Courtney has been raised on pure love by all of us. She accepts you unconsciously as her Mother right now. She feels that she needs details and confirmation. We are here to tell her the circumstances of her birth, but also to assure her of our love and your interest in her welfare. Come on

Candy (he reverted to her pet name) I am right here with you. I love you, you do know that, don't you?"

Candace looked up at him with tear filled eyes, so like her daughter's and said; I know you love me and I don't deserve your love."

"Hush Baby, we all make mistakes. We are here to resolve a serious mistake. You have to trust God to give you the strength to say the right thing. Now come with me Dear, it will not be as bad as you think."

Linda greeted them at the door with a hug for her sister and a look of inquiry for her brother. Gus nodded slightly and gently nudged Candace in the direction of a chair. He moved around behind her and as every face turned toward him. He asked God to place the right words in his mouth, then began to speak.

The family spent two emotional hours in Linda's living room. Courtney was stunned at Candace's revelation and felt a justified sense of betrayal. She wanted to believe that her mother did not want her at all. All of the adults hastened to assure her that was not the case.

Oddly enough her anger was directed at Gus. She felt that her Uncle Gus should have 'fixed' the situation and be her Daddy. She totally ignored Troy. Until recently he had been her favorite Uncle and Godfather. She did not know how to skip from Godfather to Father. She had no idea how to treat her "Mother/Aunt" Linda (oddly enough she sat down between Gus and Candace) so ignored her.

Gus finally suggested that they all go home and

meet again on Sunday afternoon. Candace cried all night and his heart hurt for her. The only thing he could do for hold her. The next move was Courtney's and the child had to be given time to absorb her new situation.

Troy called later and asked if he could come by? Gus agreed and they settled down in his study with their drinks.

"Troy started out complaining. "Why did Courtney ignore me Man? She knows I'm her Dad. I was always her favorite uncle. What do I do now? Should I speak to her? I always thought she loved me. What am I supposed to do now, Man?

For a moment Gus sat there and silently asked God; why me Lord? Why do they always come to me? I don't have any answers, so what am I to tell him? "You have to give her time Troy. Let her sort out her feelings for Linda and her feelings about Candace. She has to make a few practical decisions about her situation, then she can tackle her feelings for you. You are an entirely new part of this equation and she needs time to put you into play."

"She is angry with me and I understand that. It is not rational. She has to have someone to lash out at. She feels safe with me. I'm the Daddy. I love her unconditionally and she knows it."

"My advice to you is to take one day at a time. Look into the possibility of having your name put on her birth certificate and changing your will. You will show her that she is your only child and heir. She's smart enough to be impressed. That gesture alone tells her that you love her and acknowledges that you are her father. I have to cut this short. I have a wedding at the Temple to-morrow (as a favor for Jake), want to come and keep me company?"

"Alright, Jake's done me a lot of favors, it won't hurt to return one."

"Gus ushered Troy to the door. "Meet me at the Temple at twelve noon, okay?"

"I just need some help with the tables and chairs. It should be interesting, the mother works for Jake. I am not ask you to be the "Beau of the Ball, Troy. " You will be there to work, okay."

"Thanks Man, I will be there."

Carmen awoke at four o'clock on Saturday morning. Immediately her mind went into overdrive, making mental lists of last minute things to do and people to contact. She had completed the decorations and flowers last night.

Vanessa had made herself useful by contacting the Minister and Caterer and coordinating the schedule with them.

Luis, Chris and Hugh was in charge of the limousines, other transportation, the bar and music. They were assigned those duties because the three of them considered these chores to be "man" things. They could also handle them alone.

She hit the shower at five and as she turned the water off, she heard Shawn in her bathroom. She was

crying and throwing up. Carmen slipped into a towel
robe and hurried into Shawn's room. "What's the matter
Baby? Why are you crying?"

"I'm so sick mama, and I'm scared. I can't stop
throwing up and Cara is kicking me dead in my back. I
don't think I'm going to make it through the day. I
might as well die right now. " she cried dramatically.

"If you throw up on me, I'm going to kill you.
Get your head out of that toilet, brush your teeth and gar-
gle. Get in the shower and get downstairs quickly. You
have to get something in your stomach. Cara is probably
kicking you because you are crying and throwing up and
she's hungry. Your Daddy is making your breakfast. Go
eat and keep him out of my hair while I get dressed."

"Ma, I'm supposed to be a Queen and this is my
day. You're treating me like a child," she whined.

"Correction Miss Shawn, a mentally challenged
one at that. Now get going."

She resigned herself that this would be the order
of the day. She then went in to get dressed. She had decided to leave Vanessa and Luis with the responsibility
of getting Shawn and her attendants to the Temple. She
also decided to have the Minister perform the ceremony
there. The objective being to keep Shawn as quiet as possible. Thereby preventing a premature labor and wedding sans bride.

She left the house at twelve o'clock with her
dress bag, tote and assorted boxes and bags of wedding
paraphernalia. Bessie started and she made it to the

Temple without mishap.

Gus and Troy were opening the gates as she drove up. Gus rushed over to help her out of the car. She gave him her packages and indicated the boxes on the back seat. "There's more in the trunk Do you think the other gentleman can help you with them. By the way, good morning and thanks for your help." She smiled at him as he handed her out of the car.

"Hey Troy, help me out here. This is Mrs. Ashley, the mother of the bride and Jake's friend."

"Hel - lo, Mrs. Ashley." He extended his hand to Carmen. "I am Attorney at Law, Troy Daniels, and totally at your service." Troy was stunned by her looks. What a voice and body. I never thought pleasingly plump was voluptuous until this moment, he thought to himself. "Is this the same Mrs. Ashley that my friend here has been working with for months?"

"Hey Man, are you going to stand there staring, are you going to help me with the lady's things.""Gotcha.' Gus chuckled to himself. "She doesn't just affect me that way, but most mature res-blooded males." C'mon Man, let's help the lady get this show on the road."

The two men worked as Carmen threw out orders. In no time the Temple looked like an elegant banquet hall complete with Wedding Chapel. She turned to Troy and invited him to be her Special Guest and sit at her table. "After all, you've worked harder than some members of my family. Now you will be treated as one."

"Thanks Mrs. Ashley, but I was hired by my brother here to do maintenance and tend the bar. He may not appreciate me playing Cinderella to your guests."

"Pay him no mind. You will both come as my guests. Now go home and change into something GQ. I have a group of women coming who will be glad to just look at you."

"Hey Gus, you heard the Lady. I'm going home to change clothes.

Gus shook his head in disgust at Troy's antics. "The man was in the midst of a divorce to a woman he'd been married to forever. But, he was still ready to make a pass at the first good-looking woman he saw. "I'd better let him know that she's married, before he makes a complete fool of himself. He realized how absurd his thoughts were."

"To be honest," he berated himself, "I had almost the same reaction to her that first time, only worse. Troy's not serious, but I've fallen in love with her. Just working with her today is a pleasure. I love listening to her voice and she makes me laugh constantly. I'd better leave Troy alone, I don't want him to think I'm jealous or anything like that."

"Hello in there Gus, Gus, are you still here? Carmen was a little concerned. Gus had retreated deep in thought and she felt a bit alone and totally rejected.

"I'm right here Lady. Just lost in thought."

"I've got a penny somewhere and we have about

fifteen minutes if you need to talk."

"Okay Carmen, here's the deal. Last night our situation came to a head. Candace told Courtney the truth and oddly enough I ended up the fall guy. The child is angry and blaming me for this mess, and she is angry with her mother.

She is totally ignoring Troy and his role in this mess. Poor Linda is at a loss and is extremely hurt by Courtney's rejection, She really loves Courtney. That is the only child she will ever have. Linda is extremely hurt by Courtney's rejection, but she is trying to be patient. I suggested putting everything on hold until Courtney sorts her feelings out. Do you think there is anything else I can do at this time?"

"No, you have to give her time. Not only does the child have to reassign roles, but is she mature enough to be able to switch roles. She never had a father before, now she has a living, breathing one. You were the clos-est thing to a father she had, and the one who has always been there. Troy was a fairy godfather and not quite real as a father figure. Now he wants acceptance as a father and wants her love very much. Problem: you look and behave as the *ultimate father* to all of them. She is com-fortable with that and accepting Troy would having to give it up.

With Candace you have to find a way to make her believe that you forgive her and does not judge her. That this mistake does not diminish your love for her one bit. Truly neither of us can say that we don't understand what happened between her and Troy; we've been there and done that ourselves. You have to convince her that you sincerely understand and that human beings make mistakes. As Donnie McClurkin sings; "We fall down, but we get up.' It is time for her to ask God and you to forgive her, but she has to find a way to forgive herself first. Until she forgives herself, she will not be able to *get up*.

Take her out to dinner and buy her something beautiful. Remember the early days and find something that will bring back memories of happier days. But most of all, just be there for her. She will eventually come around. No one wants to be miserable forever. Just be patient and ready to help in whatever way she may need you." She leaned over and hugged him. "Hang in there, things will work out Okay friend?"

The quick, brief hug made Gus feel much better. He enjoyed listening to her no non-sense advice, and had every intention of taking it Meanwhile; they had a wedding to get through.

The guests began to arrive and Carmen slipped into the dressing room to change. She emerged ten minutes later in a stunning mauve, beaded gown with navy accessories. Gus' gut tightened briefly as she passed and her perfume wafted to his nose.

He shook his head and went to the men's room to change into appropriate attire for a wedding. He too caused a few female heads to turn as he crossed the floor, heading for the bar.

Roseatta and Erica were sitting together and an "I told you so look" was exchanged between them as they watched him stop to speak to Carmen.

Erica told her friend, "those two don't even know that when you are in love it shows, whether you know it or not."

The wedding was beautiful. Shawn's gown was a cleverly cut, off white empire that made her look like a chocolate Botticelli maiden. Vanessa had piled her sister's hair up in fat ringlets that cascaded over her crown and down her back in lieu of a veil. She wore her mother's good pearls with her sister's pearl earrings. The jewelry showed of her lovely neck and shoulders drawing attention away from her "extended" waistline.

The dress had cap sleeves and a deep sweetheart cleavage that showed off her luminescent shoulders and the tops of her breasts. Carmen's eyes filled as she held her beautiful baby in her aims for the last time. She was so proud as Hugh walked down the aisle with her, his head held high. He was trying to look dignified and pleased at the same time.

The Minister did his thing and to everyone's surprise and delight, asked Luis if he would like to salute his bride. Being a typical, romantic Trini, her son-in-law spoke eloquently of his love for Shawn. He also expressed his pride in his new family. He asked her parents to forgive him for bringing their daughter to the altar bearing his daughter. He promised to take the best care of them both.

The women were crying all over the room by the time he finished and of course the men were exclaiming over his machismo. The exchange of rings were anticlimatic to Luis's dramatic presentation.

Gus and Troy worked like they were being paid and had a thoroughly good time. They both agreed that Luis was a born Mason. His honor and sense of duty, and his commitment to his family was exactly the character traits fostered by Gus and his brothers.

They worked companionably along with Hugh and Luis' family members. Together they tended bar and served the guests. They also cleared up spills and corralled cute kids that had gotten loose from their parents.

This was the first time the two men had spent serious time with each other since Troy's confession They were both glad that their friendship would remain intact. Time would take care of their other issues. They were both patient men, committed to their family and wise enough to know that healing would come in time.

Hugh had the time of his life. He was so proud of his Luis. "I always knew that boy was the best thing that ever happened to this family." he told anyone who would listen to him for five minutes." He made the toast to the couple and didn't even bother to try to outdo Luis. He spoke of his love for Carmen and the pride he had in his beautiful girls.

He bragged about his two perfect son-in-laws and told his guests that now there were two sons to balance his women's influence. He expressed his gratitude to the new couple for naming their daughter for his beloved wife. He ended by toasting his new granddaughter. Everyone applauded wildly and he sat down, too pleased with himself.

Carmen told her friend Gail facetiously that was

the longest speech Hugh had ever made. She was too tired to laugh at her tipsy husband. She leaned over to her friend Charlotte and whispered; do you think he's enjoying himself?" They cracked up.

Jake had introduced him to Gus and Troy earlier as his Lodge brothers and told him that Gus was the Grand Master and responsible for getting the place for them on such short notice. Hugh thanked them both and realized after they left that Gus must have been the Chap working with Carmen on that special project. "I wonder if that was the same chap that helped her get her car started that time?"

After the reception Hugh went home with Vanessa and Chris, leaving Carmen to supervise the cleaning and packing up the leftover food, gifts and liquor. She also had to pay the Minister, Caterer, Musician, DJ and Photographer. She was exhausted and her feet and back were killing her.

Erica, Gus, Jake, Roseatta, Adam and Troy helped her load her car. Bessie of course wouldn't start. Gus tried to do his magic with the carburetor and Troy added his limited expertise. No one else had any experience with Mercedes. Here she was stuck at midnight. Her car was loaded with food and gifts and her feet seriously swollen and hurting.

"I will call Hugh and have him come for me," she told them.

"That doesn't make sense. Your husband is probably asleep by now. I will take you home. The Expedition can hold all of your things. You can call Triple

A to have it towed to your garage in the morning. Tonight you are going home."

"I am definitely too tired and miserable to argue Sir. Tomorrow it will be me and Triple A, or is it Triple A and I?"

The men transferred her things and Gus locked Bessie up for the night. "Somebody ought to do her a favor and steal it, but it probably won't start for them either," Gus muttered under his breath.

Carmen fell asleep before they reached the Jackie Robinson Parkway. Luckily Luis and Chris were in the driveway when he pulled up to the duplex. He called the young men over and said, "your mother-in-law is dead tired. You need to get her things in the house while I wake her up."

"I am awake, I am just too tired to open my eyes , or move a muscle. Again Mr. Hayden, thanks for the rescue. Do you carry an official Fair Maiden rescue card?""

"No Ma'am but I do have a rescue card for Middle Aged Matrons in busted Mercedes Benz's."

"Thank God for card carrying Black Knights. I hope things work out with your family. I will pray for you all."

"I will appreciate that. Good night Mrs. Ashley...uh Carmen."

"Goodnight Sir Augustus," Carmen laughed as

"What was that?" Chris asked Luis. As they
unloaded the Expedition.

"Shawn said it's none of our business, I guess
yours either, okay!."

"I beg to differ. I am family now," Luis laughed
at his new brother-in-law.

Carmen was mentally and physically exhausted.
She stripped out of her clothes and stepped into a scald-
ing shower. The hot water felt delicious as it sluiced
over her back. She leaned up against the shower wall
and held first one, the other foot under the water. She felt
the pain in her ankles and the soles of her feet ease a little. She thanked God for Black Knights and Four by
Fours.

She would still be waiting on Triple A if Gus
hadn't volunteered to drive her home. She was much too
tired to deal with Triple A or worry about recalcitrant old
cars now.

All she wanted was her bed, but with Hugh so
happy after a few drinks and in a celebratory mood. Trust
him to expect her to act like a dutiful wife tonight. Truthfully, he deserved some, after working so hard at his role
of Proud Papa .

On the bright side the wedding was beautiful.
Shawn made a lovely bride and she was proud to have
Luis as a son. Now that the parents were safely married,
they could all settle down and wait for baby Cara to
make her entrance and change all of their worlds. She
stepped into the bedroom and called to Hugh, Honey are

you asleep? Hugh didn't answer. She walked over to his side of the bed. He lay flat on his back gently snoring.

She quietly lay down on her side of the bed, and was asleep minutes after her head hit the pillow.

Gus drove back to Brooklyn tired but oddly enough happier than he had been in a long time. He had met so many people, many of the names familiar through Carmen's conversations. He liked her family and realized that her husband was exactly as she had described him. He also realized that the man was devoted to his wife.

He could also see that Carmen joked about her husband but that she cared deeply for him. He was smart enough to understand that the two of them had family bonds too tightly tied to be easily broken. Even by a once in a lifetime affair. Human nature was quirky enough to allow for a bit of wishful thinking on his part.

He stopped at the kitchen window and took a re-affirming look out at his moon-washed garden. He squared his shoulders and resigned himself for whatever faced him upstairs.

Chapter Eight

Two weeks later Carmen was at her desk working when Erica entered the room. "Mrs. C, have you heard from Mr. Hayden in the last few days?"

"No Erica, why do you ask?"

"Adam just called, he said that Mr. Hayden's wife was in an automobile accident last night and she's dead."

"Are you sure Erica, is Adam sure about this?"

"He's at Mr. Hayden's house now Ma'am. Mr. Ames wants to see you in his office. He's really upset."

"I'm on my way this minute." She rushed to Jake's office and found him on the phone. "Alright Troy, I'll notify the Brothers and Sisters. Give Gus my condolences and tell him we stand ready to assist in any way necessary. I'll be there as fast as I clear my desk. "Yes Man, she's right here. Just a moment."

He moved his mouth away from the receiver. "Carmen this is Troy Daniels, he needs to speak to you, is that okay?.

"Of course," She took the receiver out of his hands. "Hello Troy, is there anything I can do?"

"We need you over here. Gus said that you know what the situation is. Courtney and Linda are both devastated and the child is blaming herself. She can't stop crying and she won't let me help her. She wants her God-father, but Gus is in no shape to comfort anyone right now. His boys are here and they are not handling this well. We are in desperate in need of some organization and objectivity Asap. Can you come now?"

"I need an address and directions."

Jake spoke up, "I'll take you Carmen. I need to touch base with Gus and get the details of this tragedy."

"Let me get my purse and call home. I'll be ready in ten minutes. She rushed back to her office and called Hugh. "Honey I won't be home for awhile. Augustus Hayden's wife was killed in a car accident and Mr. Ames needs me to go over there with him to see what I can do to help. I will probably be home late., How is Shawn?"

"Shawn and Luis are in their room looking at cribs. She ate the soup I made for her. She said her back is hurting."

"Where is her back hurting Hugh?"

"I don't know you have to ask her."

"Put her on the phone, okay."

"Shawn," he yelled into the hallway. "Your Mama's on the phone."

Shawn waddled into their bedroom and fell across the bed. "Hi Ma, what's up?"

"Your Daddy said your back is hurting. Is it your lower back Baby?"

"Right now it's all over, Don't worry we'll call you if anything happens."

"Do you have my cell number?"

"Yes Ma, I've had it for five years, and before you can ask, Luis knows it too?"

" Mr. Hayden's wife just died in an accident. I'm going over there now to do what I can to help. Call me if anything happens, promise?"

"I saw that accident on TV Ma. That was some bad crash. She must have been asleep because the lady rolled right into the path of that truck. That driver couldn't have stopped if he wanted to. Is her husband the man who helped us at my wedding? Please give him a big hug from Cara and me. Tell him we are praying for him."

"I will Baby, you know he's Mr. Ames's lodge brother and good friend. I can just imagine what is going on over there in that house now.' Carmen thought to herself. "Thank God Mrs. Hayden had not suffered. That was something the family could be thankful for. Of course that thought would not bring comfort to Gus and his family right now. Her heart ached for all of them.

She picked up her bag. Carmen and Jake left the office together. He had already called his wife to tell her what had happened. He also told her that he was taking Carmen with him. They would go to his friend and do whatever they could to help. He knew he would be late getting home and didn't want her to worry.

"Thanks for driving me, I don't need to get stuck in Brooklyn tonight. Bessie is really giving me serious problems. She acted up on the way in this morning. I'm going to have to do something about her, and soon."

"I fully agree, but I understand how you feel about that car. She's like an old friend. But you have to face reality Carmen, you must realize that driving her is not safe. You break down regularly. Eventually you will find yourself in an unsafe place and you could get hurt."

"Just remember why we are here today. I am sure Gus kept Candace's car in excellent running condition. It must have been an error on her part that cost her life. But, we may never know the truth because the car was totaled. Back to you Carmen, you should have your car checked thoroughly and if you are not satisfied with the results, think about a new one. I know things are tough for you financially right now. But it's better to be safe than sorry. You are important to a lot of people and we wouldn't want to lose you."

He spoke to Carmen as they drove. " To have the life and breath of a family snatched away in an instant would be difficult in any circumstance. Given the present situation that particular family was experiencing, Candace' death at this time was particularly tragic." Jake told Carmen as they negotiated the rush hour traffic from Flushing to East Flatbush.

She also had daughters and Gus and Jake knew that she enjoyed an unusual rapport with young people. She should be able to draw Courtney out and find a way to help her during this difficult time. She knew that the child was grief stricken and may be feeling guilty and blaming herself in some way.

She knew that Jake had probably suggested that she attend the family because she was aware of the ("Courtney Situation").

As for her friend Gus, he would be suffering from a combination of emotions; helplessness and guilt. He probably blamed himself for failing his wife when she needed him most. Carmen would only be able to offer him sympathy and maybe wash a few dishes and straight -ten up the house.

Jake found a parking space near an attractive white house on the quiet, East Flatbush street. Each of them preparing in their own way to face their friend in his grief. "Our job over the next few days is to take care of this family. We will be there when they need us."

"At this point Gus may not be able to do simple things. He'll need you and Troy to help him take care of the more serious aspects of his wife's sudden death. Our presence should be helpful in the event that he need to open up and express his grief, plan a funeral and help his sons and Courtney."

She touched Jake's arm and said: "Let's go do what friends do best, be there when needed."

Jake helped her out of the car and they approached the house together. When the doorbell rang, Augustus, Jr. was in the process of trying to explain where Grandma was to little Gus and his brother Jon. He ushered them in and told them, 'Dad's upstairs with Courtney and Aunt Linda."

A voice that could only be Courtney's was screaming from somewhere upstairs. Carmen heard Gus's rumble and a female voice over the young girl's. Jake pushed her gently toward the stairs and whispered; "You can see he needs you girl, go to him."

Startled; she looked up at Jake. She only saw concern mirrored in his kindly eyes, not judgment or censure. She turned swiftly and mounted the stairs. She saw a door open at the end of the hall and moved to it.

Gus and an attractive woman about her age were there. They were standing over the bed occupied by a crying teenager that was an exact replica of the woman. "Hello Gus and you must be Linda," she said to the woman. Maybe I can help you with this situation. go on downstairs. Jake and Troy is waiting for you."

She knelt down beside the bed. Kneeling she was eye-level to the girl. "You must be Courtney, I'm Ms. Carmen. I work with Jake and Gus. I understand that you are my friend Gus's favorite god-daughter. I have two daughters of my own. I also have a nice chest that they like to lean on when we talk. Sometimes if you tell someone what is wrong, the problem is not so bad. Is there anything I can do to help?"

Gus and Linda started to speak at once, but Linda burst into tears as she tried to tell her what happened. He calmly took Linda in his arms and shushed her. "This is a friend, she has young daughters, maybe she can get through to the child. Courtney down. Come with me Linda, I'll fix you a cup of tea, and I can use a cup of coffee." He looked at Carmen and nodded toward the bed? " Please do what you can. We are all at the end of our ropes."

She turned to the young girl and nearly drowned in her huge, brown eyes brimming with tears. "Hi dear, I understand that you are my friend Gus's favorite god-daughter. May I sit down?"

The girl sniffled and nodded her head. Carmen sat down beside her on the bed. "Would you like to talk about your problem? I promise you, once you talk to me you will feel better. As she spoke she settled into a sitting position on the bed and pulled Courtney into her arms. Her arms tightened around the child and the floodgates opened. The tears fell as the child began to talk. Carmen stroked her hair as she held her.

Carmen soothed her and listened as she spilled out her pain and grief for her mother. Part of her stress was shame over the way she had treated Candace. Her mother had tried to talk to her and she had rebuffed her. Now, her Aunt Linda was her only mother and she hadn't been nice to her. What was she going to do if Aunt Linda didn't love her anymore?

Carmen held the child and let her spill out her pain and grief, and her enormous sense of guilt. She wanted to take the blame for a situation not of her mak-ing. She was angry and hurt and terribly lost. Her world had shifted and changed and she had no idea what to make of it. Carmen rocked her in her arms and let her strength be the solid wall the child needed to lean on.

Downstairs Gus took care of Linda while he kept an ear peeled for sounds from upstairs. "Don't worry Man." Jake reassured him. "The child will be fine. Carmen has a way with people, especially the young ones." The two friends sat down at the kitchen table with Young Gus, his bother Jon, Troy Linda. They discussed the arrangements for Candace' service until Jake's wife called. He hurriedly left the house and completely forgot about Carmen.

A little while later Carmen came downstairs with a hungry Courtney in tow. Only to discover that Jake had left her stranded. She spent an hour getting aquainted with the family. Gus Jr. and his wife were a charming couple and Little Gus was adorable. Jon, Jr. was a handsome young man in his mid-twenties. His girlfriend (and Jon, Jr's Mom) was obviously in love with him. She seemed to be very much a part of the family. They were all in the initial stages of grief.

All except Little Gus. He had no clue about why the grown-ups were so sad, and why no one would play with him. Jon, Jr. was a little more mature and realized that his Grandma was gone. He sat quietly in front of the television. She wasn't sure whether he was really watching it.

Carmen picked up the little boy and held him as she sat down. She chatted with the boys until she got them to respond to her. Courtney never left her side. She just needed some time to process this new development.

She would eventually come around. The girl had the resilience of youth on her side. She suggested that she would feel better once she got something to eat.

"Linda immediately sprang into action and produced a sandwich and Coke for the teenager. As they stood by the sink washing dishes, Linda softly said: thank you Carmen, I really did not know what to do. I hope to you'll come again soon."

"I'll check in with you tomorrow." It was getting late and she needed to get home. "Could someone please call a cab for me?"

Gus insisted on driving her home. He needed to get out of the house for awhile anyway. As soon as they settled her and her tote bag in the Expedition. Gus asked her; "Lady, what happened to your car? Did it break down again?"

"Actually I think that she's alright. Jake brought me here because he didn't' want to take a chance on me breaking down en route to you."

"I'm glad. I can't thank you enough for dealing with Courtney tonight. We had tried for an hour to quiet her down. We were all afraid she'd make herself sick. Linda is taking Candy's death and the child's rejection hard. Those two grew up like twins.

Right now Courtney is not thinking of her Aunt, she's only focusing on her own grief. She has decided to blame herself for Candace' death. There was nothing we could say or do to change her mind. Thank God you got through to her."

"She's young and at the place where she takes on everybody else's stuff, but can't even handle her own. We had a long talk and I promised to be here everyday for as long as she needs me. I also explained to her that her Mama Linda and I stressed the "Mama". I told her that Linda was hurt too and she could help her."

"This is a very difficult time for the family and myself. It is a blessing that none of us is responsible for Candy's death. The Coroner said that she appeared to be crying and never saw the truck coming. She died instantly and did not suffer. We have to thank God for that. We have not begun to absorb all of this. The kids are all in shock and I'm on automatic pilot. I really appreciate you and Jake, Troy too. I know he's in his own particular hell right now. Yet he is taking care of all of the legalities surrounding the accident and securing Courtney's inheritance as well."

They pulled into her driveway and Gus got out of the car. "I'm going to check your car right now. There is obviously something wrong with it."

"This is not the time for you to do mechanic work."

"Please, I need to keep myself and my thoughts busy. This will only take a few minutes. Does your husband have any tools?"

"I'll check with him." She opened the door and entered the house. "Hugh, do you have any tools? Someone is here to check the car."

"I'm watching T.V, look in the garage."

Gus found a few tools and some oil and other fluids strange to Carmen. After an hour he emerged from beneath the hood with filthy hands and smudged forearms and face. "That should hold you for now. But Lady, you need to think about another car, and soon."

"Later Sir, I have a baby on the way right now, let's get you acquainted with some hot water."

"Carmen was in and out of the two houses in East Flatbush for the next three days. She helped Linda and Andrea (Young Gus' wife) and Shannon (Jake's wife) prepare food and keep the house clean. She and the women became fast friends. She and Courtney also bonded closely. The young girl stuck to her like glue, talking incessantly. Carmen was used to young girls chatter and allowed her to use her to as a buffer.

They buried Candace in Cypress Hills Cemetery., on a beautiful Thursday afternoon. The reception was held at the Temple. Carmen, Jake's wife Shannon and Gus' Eastern Star Chapter, served the family and their friends delicious food prepared by the women.

The Matron of the chapter was a friendly and intelligent woman. She recognized immediately that Carmen was curious about the Order. She invited her to an upcoming function. She also gave her a little background on the Order of the Eastern Star.

Carmen had thought briefly about pledging a Sorority and had passed up the opportunity in college. She saw the Eastern Star as a sisterhood, but for more mature women. She agreed to attend the function.

The Friday night after the funeral Baby Cara made her entrance into the world. Carmen had taken Courtney to a teen speak out at her Church. Luis called her on her cell phone (He really did have the number). She didn't have time to drop Courtney off, so she rushed to the hospital with the teenager in tow.

This was the Courtney's first experience of a birth, so Carmen asked her if she'd like to watch. Courtney was fascinated and a future physician was born that night. Shawn also won an adoring play sister and Cara a junior god mother.

Hugh and Luis were elated. They took complete credit for the perfect doll in the crib. It helped that she was the spitting image of her Grand Daddy, right down to the fringe of hair on her little bald head.

Vanessa and Chris came in loaded down with toys and were immediately appointed Godparents. The nurse finally chased them all out of the room, except for Luis. They took their happy group into the Maternity Lounge where Luis' parents joined them. It was after ten o'clock when they went down to the parking lot. Hugh had come with Luis and decided that he would go back with him.

Vanessa and Chris headed for Staten Island and that left Carmen to drive Courtney back to Brooklyn, and then home to Queens. Bessie of course would not start. "Dammit Bessie,'. Carmen swore."You cannot let me be stuck in the middle of this hospital parking lot. I've got to get this child home." She got out of the car and looked for a security guard or maintenance man. She saw no one.

"You better get back in the car Ms. Carmen. My God Poppa says we are not ever supposed to get out of a disabled car in a dark parking lot. You better call him to come for us. I'm getting scared."

"I'm going to call Triple A." She dialed the number and went through the drill. When she finally got through, they told her she had an hour's wait. She hung up and told Courtney they would just have to wait with the car. She dialed her home and when Hugh answered told him what had happened.

"I'll see you when you get home. Don't let them mess up that front end when they tow it, you hear."

"I hear you Hugh. Courtney call your Godfather and ask him if he will come and wait with us. I'm a little right now, scared too."

Courtney dialed the number and Gus answered on the first ring. "Where are you Munchkin? Aunt Linda and I were starting to get worried."

"I'm with Ms. Carmen. Shawn had her baby and I saw it. We can't get Bessie started and Triple A says we have to wait for hours. Come get us God Poppa, please, I'm scared?"

"Stop talking so fast Baby, put Mrs. Ashley on the phone, now."

"Oh Gus, I'm sorry." Carmen apologized. Bessie won't start and we're in the Metropolitan Hospital parking lot waiting for Triple A. They said they'd be here in an hour, but you know what that means. I'm getting a little nervous and Courtney wants you."

He thought to himself, "I'll bet you do to, but is much too proud to admit you are scared of anything." He simply asked her to tell him exactly where she was. "I'll be there in fifteen minutes? If I am not there and Triple A comes, tell Courtney to call me on my cell phone, okay?"

He was already backing out of his driveway as she gave him her location. "That car has got to go, ASAP. He muttered as he hit the Jackie Robinson Parkway doing sixty. "I can't take much more of this. I'm going to talk to Troy and Jake. Between us we ought to do something for this stubborn and prideful Lady."

He pulled into the parking lot next to the decrepit Mercedes to find the woman awkwardly holding the child's head on her shoulder. They were both sound asleep.

He shook his head in dismay. "They must have scared themselves to sleep. Triple A or muggers could have towed them and Bessie away, they would never have known it." He tapped lightly on the window and two sets of startled eyes flew open.

They unlocked the door and woman and girl fell into his arms. Everybody started crying (Gus needed it as much as the women) and the healing started as the tears of relief and delayed grief fell unchecked over three sets of cheeks.

Two weeks later Carmen came downstairs to find Bessie gone from her usual parking space. "For God's sake, the car doesn't even run. Who in their right mind would steal a car that they have to push?' she fumed. "I have to get to my meeting and I am already late. I hope Bessie breaks down in front of the nearest police station. It would serve the thieves right to get caught in something that ragged."

As she stood there fussing a young man pulled up next to her. He was in a late model dark blue Mercedes. He stuck his head out of the window and called to Carmen. "Hey Ma'am. Do you know a Mrs. Ashley?"

"I'm Mrs. Ashley," she snapped ungraciously. "What do you want?"

"A gentleman asked me to deliver this car to you. He said to tell you that your car has been retired from service and that you are to enjoy the new *"Bessie"* and consider it *a "gift'* for you and *"peace of mind"* from your *Brothers Gus, Jake and Troy.* Carmen just stood there. She couldn't help the tears that began to run down her face. *(*This looked like Troy's ex-wife's old car*)*. To her it looked like brand new. This had to be the nicest thing that anyone had ever done for her in hr life.

The young man opened the door with a flourish. Carmen sank down into the supple leather seat. There was a lovely red bow tied to the rear view mirror. An envelope was attached. She opened the envelope with trembling hands and read; Thank you my Lady for the gift of your friendship.

Courtney adores you and with your guidance is beginning a natural adjustment to her unique situation. Troy is more than a little bit in love with you and loves you for guiding his daughter to him. Linda looks upon you as a "Sistah" to fill the void left by her beloved Candace. I am convinced that Jake has a serious crush on you and Little Gus says that you are the best "hugger' in the world. My sons and daughters-in-law considers you their own "Black Martha Stewart."

You have been a good friend to me and is the best thing that has come into my life for many years. I cherish our friendship and our business relationship. I don't know what the future holds, but always consider me your best friend and "Black Knight", tarnished armor and all. Please accept *"New Bessie"* in the spirit that it was given.

You deserve the best that life has to offer, because you give often and unselfishly. Allow others to give to you in the same generous and unselfish manner and above all drive safely.

Yours Always

Augustus Hayden, Sr.

Carmen was floored. She sat in the first decent car that she had ever owned and let tears of love and gratitude flow freely. As she cried, she thought of her life with Hugh. She accepted the fact that she had made a commitment to him many years ago. One that she would never, ever break.

She thought about how difficult her life had been before Hugh. He had worked hard to provide for her and the girls. Without him she would have taken longer to complete her education, and certainly would not have had the opportunity to work in the community and advance her career.

She also thought of her dreams of a "Knight". One who would treat her like a Lady and fulfill all of her sexual fantasies. Those dreams were fantasies, as ephemeral as dust. They could in no way replace thirty years of love and commitment and two daughters. God had allowed her a glimpse of what real love and sexual fulfillment should be. He had let her feel cherished and cared for by a strong, kind and compass-ionate man.

This man of her dreams had given her a complete meal, a feast of love, passion and sexual fulfillment. That feast would have to carry her through the rest of her life. But it would be enough to know what depths of emotion she was capable of. And that there was a man who could plumb those depths.

The surreal afternoon in the garden had seared their souls and melded a permanent bond between them. For as long as Carmen lived she would remember the power of his "kiss" and she would be the "Lady" of her song. She only had to close her eyes to hear him say as clearly as if he sat in the car next to her.

You are my Lady, he said to me. And I am your man for eternity. He came into my life and made me regret. Vows made to another, an older man that I can't forget. Te power of the ocean is in your kiss. His loves s real, it makes me feel, eternal bliss. "I'll change your life from pain, stress and strife. Make your dreams come true, take care of you, though you are not my wife."

She knew that she had met her "Man" for eternity. But she also realized that "eternity" for them was limited to that one magical day in Hawaii.

Eternity to them was limited to the day that they shared at the beautiful and ethereal War Memorial at Pearl Harbor. The visit to the hallowed ground of Punch Bowl Crater and the time spent in the Magical Garden in Hawaii. Eternity was also undying love, devotion and friendship; honed by two souls melding into one.

The watchwords of their relationship would have to be commitment, honor and integrity. The reality of their "Eternity" for Carmen would always be a love song written by her and inscribed on her heart.

Bonus

Selections

A short Story:

Photo Courtesy of;
Jeff Schmerling 2011

Am I Really Dreaming

A Short Story by: Jean Ferguson
Chapter 1

The young woman was stretched out on the lounge next to the Olympic sized swimming pool. She was so tightly strung the air fairly zinged with the tension emanating from her shapely body. Her eyes were squeezed tightly shut, and she appeared to be waiting for something she feared.

Suddenly a foot shot out of nowhere and kicked her in the side. The blow was so swift and hard she instantly toppled over into the pool. Her eyes opened as she hit the water and she starts to struggle. After a breathless interval, the girl righted herself and looked around in terror.

A tall, well built man around thirty years old was standing at the side of the pool. He was extremely handsome. He was dressed casually in well-cut white slacks, a navy blue, short sleeved sport shirt with shoulder tabs, and white deck shoes without socks.

His dark hair was full and slightly tousled (as though he'd gotten out of a car in the last few minutes) and hadn't bothered to run a comb through his thick, black hair. Or he spent time at an expensive hair salon.

His skin was like honey with long lashes shading tawny eyes. He blandly held out his hands for the girl who was treading water. She looked as though she'd rather drown than reach out to him. He insistently held out his hand. The girl approached and as she stepped onto the second step, his foot lashed out and struck her in the chest. She fell backward into the pool with a silent scream.

She came up out of the water. Tears were streaming down her face so hard, that you couldn't be sure where the water stopped and the tears began. She looked around for help but the only one in sight was the man. Who again held his hand out. Now she was cold as well as frightened.

She had no choice but accept his outstretched hand. This time he let her gain the third step before he backhanded her into the pool. By now she realized that she would not leave the pool alive. She swam to the opposite side only to have him reach there as she made it to the top step.

This time he kicked her squarely in her rib cage and as she fell backward into the water, blood spewed out of her mouth. The chlorinated blue water was beginning to be tinged with pink as she revived enough to swim to the steps and sprawl face down in the water on the second step. He reached down and pulled her up by her hair. He then dragged her up on the apron of the pool where she coughed and sputtered her way to consciousness.

The man's expression never changed throughout the beating He patiently waited for her to gather enough strength to move into the house. She staggered into the room off the patio and into her bedroom. She didn't even register the lovely surroundings. The room was decorated in several shades of blue. The queen-sized bed was covered with a satin comforter and dust ruffle of royal blue with matching drapes hung with white lace panels.'

The slipper chair in the corner was covered with a smoky blue grey-fabric that matched the rug on the floor. The room was decorated in several shades of blue. The slipper chair picked up all of those colors and blended them into a strikingly pretty and comforting whole. The girl fleetingly regretted never being in a state of mind to enjoy the beautiful room. To her it was a lovely prison, nothing more.

She slowly made her way to the bathroom. The pain was becoming unbearable. She turned on the shower and sat down on the commode until the pain subsided enough for her to stand under the hot spray. She lowered her head to her knees and silently prayed; The Lord is my shepherd..The Lord is my shep..herd...O Lord I'm so sorry. I can't remember your prayer. Help me Father. I'm hurting sooo...bad. I believe you hear me and won't leave me alone. I know that I just have to keep trusting you, and I will. I promise you no matter what happens, I'll keep believing in you. But Lord I really need your strength...right now Lord...Amen.

She saw the tawny eyes watching her, and slowly straightened up. The man just stood there, watching her. The girl got up slowly and walked around him to the shower. She stepped under the spray and with much difficulty pulled and tugged the wet bathing suit from her aching and bruised body. His eyes never left her. She tossed the suit into a corner of the stall and attempted to pull the shower curtain closed. He knocked her hand away and stood there silently watching her.

She turned her back and let the hot water wash over her. His eyes on her made her feel dirty and vulnerable. She tried to scrub the feeling away with the hot water and soap. The girl only succeeded in irritating her lovely, cocoa colored skin. The water could never, ever cleanse the feel of his hands on her flesh

Chills ran up her spine in anticipation of the horror waiting her on the other side of the shower wall. After she could delay no longer, the young girl stepped out of the shower and reached for the bath sheet hanging on the door. He snatched it out of her hands and proceeded to dry her tenderly. Taking care to rub her in the most personal areas intimately. She fought back her tears. She knew from experience that tears enraged him. He would now resort to new heights of torture.

As he drew her to the bed, she could feel the angry lust oozing out of his pores. She was so frightened that her legs refused to propel her forward. The man picked her up in his arms and held her head tightly to his chest. His hand cradled her neck. Her mind went blank. It would not allow her to witness the coming rape and degradation of her body and retain her sanity.

Chapter Two

The photographer moved around rapidly shooting his camera. He shouted rapid instructions to the beautiful black model on the podium. The set was stark. A black backdrop hung behind a chaise lounge covered in zebra-striped fabric. A white carpet was spread beneath. carpet was spread beneath. The lovely beauty positioned on the sofa was the focus of all the activity in the room. She was simply dressed in a white bikini, her body oiled until it glowed. Her shoulder length sable hair barely moved, as she gingerly changed positions on command.

The photographer moved around rapidly shooting his camera. He shouted instructions to the beautiful model on the podium. The set was stark. A black backdrop hung behind a chaise lounge covered in zebra-striped fabric. A white carpet was spread beneath.

"Move beautiful", the photographer barked. "Swing your legs to the right. Move your torso as if a playful lover is tickling your ribs. As if he's nuzzling your navel and you can hardly bear the exquisite sensation. Give me some hair. Give me some feeling."

"She is barely moving", he thought to himself. This Chick acts as though every move hurts her. If I didn't know better, I'd think something was wrong. Her husband said she was a little strange. I have to admit she seems all right to me mentally but she is definitely hurting physically."

"Okay Baby," he crooned as he grabbed her arm to position her. "Hold it like this for me. Just for a minute, okay." She twisted and turned. She moved her hair. She looked sultry and demure by turn, but her heart was bursting with the exertion and she was sure she'd pass out looked out any minute. She could not afford to let the photographer know of her pain. She knew he wouldn't understand or believe her. Her husband made sure that everyone she came in contact with thought she was more than a little strange, albeit a good actress.

He's getting more violent and inventive by the day. She

She knew that it was only a matter of time. Eventually he would go further than her body could endure. She was beginning to accept the inevitability of her own mortality. The girl could not know that the camera lens were capturing her every facial expression on film. That the photographer was desperately trying to read her mind. Somehow he knew there was something terribly wrong and was trying to reach out to her.

The camera caught that fleeting expression of was despair. He saw the light die in her eyes. and wondered just how it would end and when. Suddenly the air in the room was charged with a peculiar energy. The charge was only felt by the two of them. It was as if her husband's presence in her life was negated, from that moment on.

The shoot ended and her husband came to collect her. She turned her head and silently looked back at the photographer as if to say "Goodbye." The photographer's gaze said silently; "So long Beauty, I heard you and I will always be with you."

The crowd was so huge it threatened to spill over the police barricades. The crescendo of the screams grew each time a car pulled up to the canopied and red carpeted entrance. The rich, beautiful and famous alighted their limousines waving and nodding to the crowd.

A very famous model turned TV sitcom star flashed her famous smile. Her husband held her arm and resigned himself to another evening of being the Star's spouse. And a famous Athlete/Sportscaster/Actor waved as he held tightly on to the arm of his Trainer/Lover.

The stars and their escorts came in. They were clothed in a brilliant swirl of expensive clothes and jewels. And enveloped in a cloud of expensive designer scents. The crowd went wild as the beautiful model/actress and her husband drove up in the black Mercedes limousine. He stepped out of the car and held his hand out to her. She hesitated a fraction of a second. That moment of hesitation was caught on film by one of the photographers in the crowd.

He pushed his way closer in order to catch every nuance of her expressions. The young woman held herself gingerly and to his trained eye could see that she moved with sheer willpower. He could feel the pain that she held leashed within her body.

Another photographer yelled. "Turn your head this way." As she did the lens of the camera caught the overwhelming pain and despair in those big brown eyes. The photographer could feel her pain. His instincts told him that she was at the breaking point. He felt I his gut that this was it. Someone had to save this beauty from the evil holding on to her arm. Someone had to save her soon.

He turned and fought his way through the crowd. He decided to go to her home and wait for them there. He had to find a way in before they returned. He sped through the busy streets as if his own life was at stake. Indeed he knew in his heart that she was his life. If she died, so would he.

Chapter Three

Minutes later he stopped his car in front of the imposing gates. The brick wall in front of him extended early a block down the street in both directions. It was at least six feet tall with jagged topped with jagged shards of glass. A gatehouse stood sentinel at the gate but did not appear occupied. It followed that there would be few servants as the man would not want witnesses to what he was now convinced was torture and imprisonment, to say the least.

He rang the bell to see what would happen, or if if there was anyone at home. A woman's voice came through the intercom above his head: Whom do you wish to see?' she asked. The photographer looked steadily at the woman and refused to break eye contact. When it became apparent that she was uncomfortable with his stare. He said to her; I recently took some photographs of your mistress. I believe that she may need them to-night. I'm sure she won't mind if you let me in to wait for her. She may even need me for more shots.

You do see what I'm telling you, don't you? He never let go of her eyes during his contrived speech. He tried hard to communicate his concern for her Mistress with his innocuous words and body language. I got the impression that her husband may not appreciate me messing up these shots.

The man might have listening devices or cameras planted. He certainly couldn't take a chance on a stranger mistakenly observing his brutality. The photo-

- graphers unspoken query about security was answered
by the maid. She silently took his hand and led him over
to an elaborate Chinese screen . Behind it was some very
expensive and sophisticated surveillance equipment. The
maid put her fingers to her lips and led him past the glass
doors of the patio. They glided through the living room
to the beautiful, blue bedroom.

The bedroom fascinated him. It was beautiful
and totally impersonal. He sensed that evil resided there.
He also sensed that the young woman would die there if
he did not intervene. The maid motioned to him to follow
her into the bathroom. Once inside she turned on the
faucets in the sink and tub.

"I must speak to you now. There is no more time
for my beautiful Mistress. The Master has terrible plans
for her tonight. He left rope in the bedroom and asked
for a rubber sheet and lots of towels. I think he plans to
kill her. You must help me save her. There is no one
else."
"Why does he want her dead? She's more valu-
able to him alive. Tell me what you know about him and
why he hates her so."

"The Mistress supports him. She works so hard
to give him everything he needs. He hates her for it. He
is good-looking and charming but she is beautiful with
real talent. He needs to totally dominate, dehumanize
and demoralize her. That is the way he has maintained
his power over her. He brutalizes her but still expect her
to worship him and respond to him sexually.

He's stripped her down to the lowest level for a
human being possible. He expects her to perform like a

trained dog and has done everything but destroy her. that is the way he maintains his power over her. He brutalizes her, but still expect her to worship him and respond to him sexually.

He has done everything but kill her body physically. Her spirit is already gone. I'm so afraid for her. She has nothing left to be afraid of afraid. Every time they attend a function where she is the center of attention, he' goes off o her and brutalize her as punishment for the attention she gets as a star.

The maid placed her hand over her mouth. "Hush I hear someone coming." He quickly and silently stepped into the closet and closed the door. The maid silently left the room.

The young woman that came into the room was a breath taking vision of loveliness. The off-white jersey gown hugged her body to perfection. The cowl neckline lovingly embraced her full breasts, and swept around her flawless shoulders to join in a floppy bow above her hips. Four inch heels showed off her shapely legs to perfection. But something was wrong. The woman advanced into the room gingerly as though it hurt to move. The man walked close behind her.

He reached out to her, but she flinched away. He grabbed her roughly and shoved her, she fell backward onto the bed. She struggled to get up but he easily held her down with one hand.

He grabbed the neck of the dress and ripped it from her shoulder. Her breasts were exposed in a skimpy push-up bra. Even as she struggled, he roughly

161

pushed her dress down over her ample hips. Suddenly he Slapped her across the face, called her names and cursed her viciously. She started to cry and he slapped her so hard her head hit the headboard with a hard crack. Her head fell to the side as she lost consciousness.

The photographer was silently snapping pictures with his zoom lenses. He was beside himself with fear. But he knew that he had to keep his composure. One sound could expose him. He knew that they both would die if he was discovered. He watched he carefully. Her chest was rising and falling with each breath. "Please God don't let her die. Please give me a chance to save her. I know you placed me here. Please, please let me do your will," amen.

The man reached under the bed and retrieved the bonds he'd left there earlier. He muttered to himself . as he worked to secured the bonds; "she won't humiliate me again, the Bitch. I'll show her just as I showed the others. I'm just as good as she is. She won't have to take care of me. I'm going to take care of her this time. I don't care what Mama says." He ran her hands caressingly over her body.

As she regained consciousness the girl began to thrash about. He held her down with one hand, then reached under the bed for the hunting knife he'd left there earlier. He held it up to the light and tested the blade by running it over her belly A thin line of blood sprang up in it's path. He pushed her head back and exposed her throat. Her eyes flew open. She implored him with her eyes to let her go. He threw his head back and laughed. He kissed her neck and followed the trail of kisses with the knife. Another line of blood sprang up.

with the knife. Another line of blood sprang up. The girl was terrified.

The photographer hidden in the closet could feel her fear. He knew that it was only a matter of minutes before the man made the fatal thrust. He eased his way to the door of the closet, preparing to take that final, fatal shot.

As he raised his camera, the man raised the knife and slashed her leg. The young woman lost consciousness. The man raised the knife again. As he brought it down, the photographer brought the camera down as hard as he could on the back of his head. The man shook his head and raised the knife to slash at the photographer. The photographer brought the camera down again as hard as possible. This time the man went down.

The photographer swiftly lifted him across his shoulders in a fireman's carry. He went through the living room to the patio door's carelessly left open. He calmly walked over to the pool and dropped his burden over the edge. The photographer stood and watched the man drop to the bottom. He traced the red rivulets of blood as they undulated through the water until they bled into the chlorinated blue.

He made his way back through the house to the bedroom. The woman was still out cold. The photographer picked up his camera and looked toward the bed. "You are safe now my Beauty. I took care of him forever. When you awake he'll be gone. You will only see him in your dreams. He cast one last look filled with love toward the "object of his protection" lying on the bed and exited the room.

The maid was patiently waiting for him at the door. "She's safe now. Her life has been spared. Go check the pool and call the police. Leave her as she is until they arrive. Forget that I was here and that you saw me."

"I never see any one or anything that happens in this house. She will be all right. I'm here for her." She opened the door and saw him out. The woman nodded her head with satisfaction.

I opened my eyes and felt that I was in the room with the young woman, the man and the photographer; Am I Really Dreaming? Could the young woman somehow be me in my first violent and abusive marriage? Did I have a bad dream caused by indigestion? Did I see something or hear something that triggered a subconscious reenactment of an event too painful to recall?

Could I have buried the scars of that violent marriage deep in my conscious. And now they are fighting to surface and be dealt with? Is it possible that the self - help groups, psychotherapy and religion didn't quite do the job of healing?

The subconscious may be doing a job for me through my dreams and bringing resolution and closure to those issues that I could not deal with up front.

I don't know the answer. I only hope that my psyche was handing me justice. Justice that I had prayed so hard for all of those miserable, painful and despairing years. Justice for the emotional deprivation, loss of self esteem and pride. Loss of sleep, broken bones. Also the total demoralization of that child/woman so long ago.

Some

of

Imogene's

Pearls"

for

Your

Enjoyment

DREAMFIELDS

With: Christina Baldwin-El.

She sits regally alone, on top of a hill.
Gazing upon her gives one quite a thrill.
Facing the Caribbean Sea , so blue.
Her graceful lines are classic and true.
A house you say, but I think not.
A concept, a dream, is more on the dot.
He wanted to give, this woman he loved.
Something precious to him'
Straight form Heaven above.
Something built for his hands.
and the sweat of his brow.
Something tangible and real,
That belonged to her now.
A monument to a relationship,
To love and respect.
A pace of contentment,
Of peace and of rest.
A gift of far vistas ad tumbling clouds.
Of twinkling stars and magic ships wrapped in
shrouds.
Some who gaze up at the top of the hill.
Al they see is a house, but I see Dreamfields.

Life Style

It's amazing, don't you think.
Tat on Saturday I can luncheon with the Links.
I never dreamed that the day would come,
When the Hyatt and Marriot, I could call home.
To spend a few nights or several hours.
Hobnob with friends and acquaintances' in
power.
To participate in silent auctions of art, and sign
my own books and become a part;
of the program of that important day and accept
the well wishes that will come my way.
What a change in my life style, from working
and worrying all the while.
I now spend most of my days in the sun,
completing the tasks that need to be done.
God has blessed me in so many ways,
I will be grateful, all of my days.
No longer to worry all he while, just to relax and
enjoy my great life-style.
I thank Him for the gifts of intelligence, good
health much love.
Sent down here to me from Heaven above.

She Is Worthy of My Tears

With Lovell Brady

Eileen married me forty years ago,
We established a family as those stories go.
She was loving and cheerful, bright and smart'
A real Christian woman, the center of my heart.
Her heart was as large as the great outdoors
Her spirit connected to mine and yours.
My Eileen lived as a good Christian aught,
Serving the Lord was a very big part.
A part of who she was and her place here on
earth. A part of God's plan for her from birth.
She has brought me great joy, and has quieted
my fears. Her passing has pulled from my eyes
the tears.
Tears of pain, of loss, and of grief,
Tears of joy and tears of relief.
My angel is now resting in her new home above,
And she will always be worthy
of my tears and love.

Happy Birthday Sweet Lady

With Andrew Henderson

Happy Birthday, Sweet Lady,
enjoy this your day.
My love and good wishes are
coming your way.
We are all gathered here,
to celebrate with you.
We'll have good food,
great fun and music too.
You are my world,
and I am so glad to share;
you with my friends;
who also care.
This is a wonderful moment in time,
To celebrate with you the tie that binds.
I love you, Sweet Lady.
with all of my heart.
And I will be with you,
Until the day we part.

Love's Color Blind

Black militant,
White Missionary?
I've often wondered, how love unfolds,
Between two such people,
so unlikely to behold.
How a "serious black militant",
Can find a "white saint",
Fall into his arms and not in a faint.
Our militant woman, believes in what's right.
Her Christian missionary,
carries on God's fight.
They are both here,
To make this world a better place.
To live in peace,
With God's good grace.
My cousin Peter loves Debbie dearly,
And she returns his love quite clearly.
They settled down,
A family to raise.
And their house rings;
out with songs of praise,
To my dear cousins',
Life has sure been kind.
For where love resides,
there is peace of mind.

Jannine

By: Jon Baldwin

I love my Jamaica,
warm water so blue.
but true paradise,
is being with you.
Since the day that we met,
I cannot resist.
But imagine our future,
together in bliss.
In the midst of life's storms,
You provide calm.
No man has the power,
To resist your charm.
My world is much brighter ,
Than ten thousand suns.
Since my souls been inspired
by hopes of your love.
Your smile has more value,
than diamonds or gold.
Your spirit embodies
A greatness of old.
My American goddess.
my precious Janine.

Chance Encounters

A visit to my doctor,
To take a test for stress.

I met a kindred sister,
as I sat down to rest.

We had shared experiences,
with our friends and family.

Our chat about the things of life,
diminishes our differences.

Oh what burdens, Mom's must bear.
They hurt much less, when we can share.

A chance encounter,
our shared grief.

Delighted my senses,
and brought some relief.

Previews
Can two people afraid of love dare to seek happiness together?

JAYNE: Imogene's first novel is a fictional accounting of Imogene's life. Jayne Longbridge is a forty-year old black woman who has escaped an abusive and violent husband. She has managed to raise four children virtually alone, acquire an education and secure gainful employment.

She is active in her church and community. She is popular, well-liked and has a sister and best friend giving that shares her life and her children.

Jason Court is fifty, successful and distinguished. He is instantly smitten with Jayne's big eyes, luscious body and air of vulnerability. And he is looking for a woman to share his life.

He sets out to woo and win her. Before they can be happy together, they will have to deal with her ex-husband, his ex-fiancée and her fears and self-doubt.

Jason builds Dreamfields, a lovely home in Jamaica and takes her there to propose.

Will she recognize Jason as the answer to her prayers, put the past behind her and accept his proposal?

Will Jason be flexible enough to deal with Jayne's crowded life?

What secret is she keeping from him and how will it ultimately affect their relationship?

Review (JAYNE)

An old fashioned love story with romance and true intimacy. You are immediately caught up and you are rooting for Jayne and Jason. Every woman wants...and needs a Jason. The characters are genuine. They touch something deep within? Perhaps some secret yearning? The author paints a vivid picture of a woman wit inner and outer strength. She is a survivor who is coming into her own. She is someone you would like to have in your life.

Florence Graydon,
Jamaica, NY

Reviews

Amazing; When I read "Pearls" I was floored by it's intensity. When I came upon the poem "You Are My Lady" it was Love, Love, Love anew. When Ms. Jayne (Imogene) asked me to sing the song I couldn't wait to get into the studio. You Are My Lady is majestic thank you Imogene for allowing me to join you on this trip."

Robert "Hi-Hat Carter

When *imogene* writes, you don't have to *imagine* anything... But... want to be a *fly* on the wall. A *voyeur* on the lives and actions of her characters. The men are hot and the women sensual... activating our carefully hidden and controlled Self.

Read and enjoy the small print and not "too" hidden messages and innuendos.

celiaW/haarlem

Review (You Are My Lady

Amazing; When I read "Pearls" I was floored by it's intensity. When I came upon the poem "You Are My Lady" it was Love, Love, Love anew. When Ms. Jayne (Imogene) asked me to sing the song I couldn't wait to get into the studio. You Are My Lady is magnetic.

The story is a classic romance tale with a twist. The ending is completely unexpected.

The setting for the love scenes are majestic and deserved to be set to music"

Thank you Imogene for allowing me to join you on this trip.

Robert "Hi-Hat Carter

"Is she in my closet or a fly on the wall?"
Celia "Afia" Wickham

"This short story was great. Once again Jean Ferguson turns one's interests to several levels at once, Stacking them like an ice cream cone with several flavors. Each flavor blending into the other, making one want just one more delectable lick."

Frank Bell Caseworker

Other Titles by Dreamfields

Coming Soon:

PURE IMOGENE"s
Perspective's and
Pearls). Imogene's
(Uncensored Auto-
biography

Imogene's 1st Novel explores relationships within a Brooklyn, NY working

CD Poetry Collection by:
Jean Ferguson
You Are My Lady (Vocals   By Gwen Johnson &
(High Hat) Carter
Music by High Hat Carter

DREAMFIELDS/ The CD
Songs written & composed by Eric & Imogene Ferguson
***

All Aboard Imogene's
Gospel Train (CD)
Arranged by: Robert "Hi Hat" Carter

Jayne and Memories of Mary Pickett and

are available online at Lightning Source.

You Are My Lady and Pure Imogene's Pearls and

Perspectives' are available at Amazon.com.

www.ingramcontent.com/pod-product-compliance
Lightning Source LLC
Chambersburg PA
CBHW060115260626
47160CB00005B/1892